Coincidences

Jean M. Ritchey

Coincidences

Joan (Michalke) Ritchey

DANCING MOON PRESS
NEWPORT, OREGON

Coincidences
copyright © Joan (Michalke) Ritchey, 2015
All rights reserved

Paperback ISBN: 978-1-937493-82-0
Ebook ISBN: 978-1-937493-83-7
Library of Congress Control Number: 2015949532

Ritchey, Joan (Michalke)
Coincidences
1. Mystery-fiction; 2. Family Secrets-fiction; 3. US Road Trip-
fiction; I. TITLE

Cover design & production: Sarah Gayle, SolaLuna Studios
Editing, book design & production: Carla Perry, Dancing Moon Press
Manufactured in the United States of America

DANCING MOON PRESS
P.O. Box 832, Newport, OR 97365
541-574-7708
www.dancingmoonpress.com
info@dancingmoonpress.com

FIRST EDITION

DEDICATION

A special thank you
to my daughter, Karen Wagner
for all the time she spent
in helping to edit this story.

I also dedicate this book to all those people who have a story to tell—fiction or non-fiction—but are hesitant to take on the challenge. The fun of creating the characters (their voices and personalities) is a gift not to be wasted. WRITE YOUR STORY!

Also by Joan (Michalke) Ritchey

poetry
From Him... Through My Fingertips
(AuthorHouse, 2008

fiction
The Brooch (A Novella)
(Dancing Moon Press, 2012)

true & fictional short stories & poetry
Captured Reflections
(Dancing Moon Press, 2015)

CONTENTS

COINCIDENCES

"Coincidence is God's way of remaining anonymous."
—Albert Einstein

ABOUT THE NOVEL:

Kathryn Carlson's gift to her granddaughter, Myndi, for her college graduation is an all-expense-paid road trip for Myndi and her dog, Ginger. It is Grandma Kate's wish that Myndi's journey include numerous historic places throughout the Western United States. The gift is a trip Myndi's grandmother had always longed to take for herself.

Myndi is excited about the adventure because she is scheduled to begin teaching classes in sixth-grade geography in September, and exploring the historic sites will provide her with firsthand knowledge to share with the kids.

A series of odd coincidences occur along the route that Grandma Kate helped Myndi plan—a journey that eventually leads Myndi to solve a secret that festered for a quarter of a century.

CHAPTER ONE:

MYNDI'S GRADUATION

MYNDI REACHED DOWN AND RUBBED the four-inch scar on her upper left thigh—a constant reminder of the accident that took the lives of her parents and three-year-old brother, Bobby. Myndi had been only five years old when she became an orphan.

"Oh, how I wish you were all here today to celebrate my college graduation with me," Myndi said to the framed photograph of her missing family. She kept the photo on her vanity table.

Ever since she could remember, Myndi had dreamed of becoming a teacher and now, with the four-year scholarship awarded her for college, and the insurance money from the accident that her grandparents had put aside for her, her dream had come to fruition.

Sitting in front of her vanity mirror, Myndi brushed her long auburn hair, letting it fall around her shoulders, framing her oval face, accentuating the dark brown color of her eyes. Staring at her reflection, and then back at the photo of her parents, Myndi thought about her facial features and how closely she resembled her mother.

Tears brimmed Myndi's eyes as she recalled her last weekend together with her parents and Bobby, and the fun they had during their stay at the beach. But she did not remember the car accident that had occurred on their way back home that Sunday. She only knew what she had been told by others, and by reading the front-page newspaper article years later.

Five-year-old Myndi Carlson is the sole survivor of a family of four, from an automobile accident on Highway 18 Sunday evening. She was life-flighted to a Lincoln City hospital in critical condition. Her parents, Franklin and Laura Carlson, and her brother, Bobby, age three, were killed instantly when a pickup truck crossed the center line, hitting the Carlson automobile head-on. The driver of the pickup was taken by ambulance to the same hospital and released later that evening.

Myndi learned that she had been thrown several feet from the car after the back door sprung open at the time of impact. Her left leg had been severely broken in two places; one was a compound fracture. She lay unconscious in the hospital for two days and woke to find a doctor, two nurses, and her grandparents standing beside her bed.

Myndi was grateful that the two years of therapy, after many operations, had left her with only a slight limp that, most of the time, was undetectable by others.

She thought again about her grandfather, Frank, and her grandmother, Kathryn, and how devastated it must have been when her father, Franklin, their only son, was killed.

Grandma Kathryn told her about the arrival of

the two police officers that Sunday evening in 1992. They explained that a tragic accident had taken the lives of their son, daughter-in-law, and their grandson. Then they offered to rush her to the hospital in their police car so she could be with Myndi when she woke up.

Myndi loved her grandparents and was so happy when, after the several-month-long court proceedings, they were finally granted custody, and one year later, her permanent adoption.

Myndi's left hand had just reached up to freshen her mascara when a flash of light streaked across the mirror. The beam of light entering through the window was a warm May sunray that landed on the diamond in the ring she was wearing. The stone cast a rainbow reflection in front of her. Her thoughts turned to Jeff and the reason for the entry she had made in her journal the night before.

Saturday—May 24, 2014

To celebrate my graduation, Jeff took me to an expensive restaurant for dinner. Our corner table by the window overlooked the downtown city lights and their reflection in the shimmering waters of the Willamette River beyond. The candlelit table setting and the ambience of the strolling violinist added to the warm glow I was feeling. It was so romantic.

To accompany the prime rib dinner, Jeff ordered our favorite wine. He was unusually quiet, but I quickly dismissed the thought when I gazed into his twinkling blue eyes and returned his smile. We were enjoying the fresh Oregon strawberry shortcake for dessert when the violinist returned to our table and played one of our favorite songs. Then the waiter and several waitresses arrived at our table with a bouquet of long-stemmed red roses in a tall fluted Mother of Pearl vase.

As I reached to summon the aroma of the flowers, I spotted a small scarlet-colored, velvet box tucked neatly among the blooms (Jeff said later how he enjoyed the quizzical glance I gave him and the shy grin that curled the corners of my mouth).

I carefully lifted the monogrammed box from its resting place and tried to calm the butterflies in my stomach. It was then that I saw my name engraved in gold lettering encircled within two intertwining hearts on the box. Jeff was sitting back in his chair. He seemed to be enjoying the range of emotions I was going through.

I had an idea of what the box held, but before I could open it, Jeff came around to my side of the table, got down on his right knee, took my hand in his and said, 'Myndi, I've loved you since grade school. I can't imagine living my life without you. Will you marry me?' I knew how Jeff felt about me—I'd sensed it for some time. My feelings have echoed his (perhaps even longer). I was beside myself with joy and surprised when I heard my voice squeak as I answered his proposal with, 'Oh, yes, Jeff. I will be your wife.' I was oblivious to the other customers in the restaurant, but when I spoke, the people at surrounding tables clapped and shouted congratulations.

Jeff was smiling broadly by then and the tension in his furled brow relaxed as he returned to his chair. He sat back, sighed, and watched while I flicked open the box.

Seated on the blue satin cushion in the center of the box was a sparkling diamond engagement ring. A heart-shaped ruby was set on each side of the center diamond. Engraved on the inside of the gold band were our names, 'Myndi/Jeff.'

Jeff reached across the table and, holding my hand, slipped the ring on my shaking finger and gently brushed away a tear of happiness as I nodded my 'yes.'

Jeff was two years older than Myndi. He'd graduated from college in 2012 and accepted a job as an apprentice in a law firm near their hometown of Tri-Mountains, a suburb of Portland. The law firm had taken an interest in Jeff and his college accomplishments after interviewing him at a job fair in his senior year. They offered him a scholarship toward his three-year post-graduate study with the hope that he would join their law office after acquiring his degree and passing his bar exams.

Myndi's thoughts returned to her preparations, but were interrupted when her grandmother entered the room. "Well, Miss Myndi Carlson, are you ready to go to the auditorium? Jeff is downstairs waiting for us, honey. This is a big day for you." Kathryn smiled at Myndi's reflection in the mirror as she squeezed her granddaughter's shoulder.

Myndi glanced up, returned her grandmother's smile, and answered, "Oh, yes! I'm so excited and ready, Gram." Then, rising from her chair, she lightly kissed her grandmother's forehead before taking her hand to descend the stairs to join Jeff.

After the graduation ceremony, Grandma Kathryn said she'd planned a surprise picnic for Myndi. By the time the three of them arrived back home, friends had already set up everything for an outdoor barbecue. It was a warm, sunny day and the flower borders circling the backyard filled the air with sweet aromas that added to the celebration.

Grandma Kathryn's gift to Myndi was a Honda Civic 4-door EX sedan. She knew Myndi's favorite color was red, so Jeff helped her select the "Tango Red Pearl" exterior color. The car had a gray leather interior with bucket seats in front and a bench seat in back. It was equipped with air conditioning, a three-disc CD system, power steering and brakes, automatic adjustable seats, and air bags.

Her grandmother had thought of everything.

The car had been a demo and registered several thousand miles, but it was equipped with an innovative experimental feature. A "navigation package" allowed the driver to address the system by voice and inquire about directions, road conditions, and miles to any specified location.

When an inquiry was made, an animated computer voice from the audio system would relate the distance and directions to a desired location.

When they entered her grandparent's house, Myndi was greeted with shouts of 'Surprise!' And that's when her grandmother presented her with the keys to the red Honda. Myndi was overwhelmed and wondered, *How did Grandma Kate know of my desire for this very car?* She thought she'd been secretive about the brochures she had kept hidden.

"Oh, Grandma!" Myndi gasped. "I saw the car parked down the street when we returned from my graduation ceremony, but I didn't give it much thought because of the sight of all the other parked vehicles. How can I ever thank you? I love you, Grandma." A few tears formed as she hugged her grandmother.

But, Grandma Kathryn's surprises for Myndi did not end with the presentation of the car....

"Myndi, I have a gift card in the amount of five thousand dollars for you as well. But that comes with one stipulation...."

By then, all the guests were at full attention.

"I'd like you to spend the money taking a three-week tour to the great sites of the United States. My wish is that while you're on the trip, you'll send postcards home to me from the places you visit. Your trip, honey, will be one I've always wanted to take, but somehow through the years just never, for one reason or another, had the time to do it. Grandpa and I were too busy, I guess." She smiled. "Anyway, it will be so nice for me to live the trip through your travels, your journals, and the postcards home."

"Grandma, why don't you come with me on the trip?" Myndi broke in.

"No, Myndi. I'd like you to take the trip by yourself, before settling into your teaching career in September, and before your wedding to Jeff next June. But I do think it would be fun for you to take Ginger along with you for company."

Ginger was a small dog weighing only twenty-pounds. Myndi had received her as a birthday gift from her grandparents when Ginger was a puppy, just a few months before the death of Grandfather Frank. Ginger was a mixture of breeds the people at the Animal Shelter could not quite identify. Her coloring was like milk chocolate, so Myndi thought it fitting to name her puppy after a spice. Ginger loved being with Myndi and loved riding in a car, especially cuddled on the green fleece blanket in the back window of Myndi's old car.

Grandma had consulted with Jeff about graduation gifts for Myndi and so he knew the plan and was happy Myndi would be taking the trip.

"My focus right now," Jeff said to Grandma Kate a few days before Myndi's party, "is on my post-graduate schooling and working part-time in the law firm. The trip really sounds exciting, but it is out of the question for me due to our plans to wed next June. Besides, I'm really motivated to save enough money to finance a down-payment on our first home."

During the next few days, Myndi and Kate spent time together mapping out a route and researching the tourist attractions that interested Myndi the most. She happily accepted her grandmother's help and enthusiasm in planning the itinerary that would include places her grandmother had particularly longed to visit. Myndi also picked out sites that would be of special interest to the students she would be teaching in her sixth grade geography classes in the fall.

Myndi was relishing this special time with her grandmother as they sipped ice-cold lemonade in the backyard shade.

Myndi smiled as she watched her grandmother trace routes with her finger while they examined the road atlas, state maps, and brochures they'd spread out on the picnic table.

One afternoon, when again reviewing travel plans, a sudden gust of wind flipped several pages of the atlas backward from Yellowstone Park in Montana to the Colorado map page. An eerie, unexplainable feeling came over Myndi as the name "Steamboat Springs" jumped out at her in a bold italic print that, for a moment, seemed to dance on the page. She glanced at her grandmother to get her reaction, but it was obvious Kate had not observed what Myndi had just experienced. In fact, she had apparently dozed off.

Myndi quickly flipped the pages back to the Montana map and planned the remainder of her route to Yellowstone.

That evening after supper, Myndi presented Jeff with the finished itinerary.

CHAPTER TWO:

MYNDI'S JOURNEY BEGINS

EARLY, ON THE MORNING OF JUNE 15, Myndi placed a new taffy-colored fleece blanket on the rear window ledge of the car for Ginger. Most of the time, Myndi was the only one able to recognize Ginger's smile. And when Ginger jumped into the back seat of the red Honda, stretched out and snuggled onto her blanket... Myndi caught that grin.

It was 6 o'clock in the morning. The sun had been up for at least an hour. "What a beautiful day to begin our trip, huh, Ginger?" Myndi nodded toward Ginger as she put a couple of overnight suitcases and Ginger's food and water bowls on the floor of the car's back seat.

Myndi had just finished loading the last of her luggage into the trunk when Jeff arrived.

"I found this leather-bound book at the office supply store yesterday, Myndi. The gold etched words on the front, *Travel Journal*, seemed to have your name written all over it. I know you keep a daily journal, but I thought we'd all enjoy reading your travel notes when you get back." Jeff smiled. "Just a little going away gift for my girl."

"Oh, Jeff. What a beautiful gift. That's a neat idea, too. It's so special, not at all like the spiral notebooks I usually use." Myndi smiled at Jeff and then gave him a lingering kiss and embrace. "I'm going to miss you, Jeff. I wish you were coming along. I love you so much, honey. Grandma was so wonderful for thinking all this through. She's looking forward to the postcards."

With a final hug and kiss for her grandmother and Jeff, Myndi and Ginger set off on their trip.

The first leg of the journey routed Myndi out of Portland and through the historic town of Troutdale, then onto the Historic Columbia River Highway. Their first stop was Multnomah Falls.

Myndi had intentionally bypassed Interstate 84

---

along the Columbia River. She'd traveled that highway many times and loved the beauty of the river, but she had never driven the old scenic Columbia Gorge highway. Guidebooks stated she would get closer views of the many waterfalls by taking this route. On other drives, she had seen only far off glimpses of Bridal Veil and Horsetail Falls. She knew when she routed her course this way that the old highway, with its many curves, would probably take a good two to three hours longer, but she planned to go slow and see it all. Picture taking was high on her list of things to do along the way, and she'd packed an extra memory disk for her digital camera. This route east was touted as especially picturesque, with several pull-off viewpoints. Of course, she would have to stop at Vista House and the lookout station at Crown Point.

In Myndi's teen years, Grandpa Frank had told her about the work he'd done in the late 1930s and early 1940s for the Works Progress Administration, which he referred to as the WPA. "The program was administered during the presidency of Franklin D.

Roosevelt and provided training and wages to unemployed men at the end of the Great Depression. I was sure thankful for the job," her grandfather said.

As she drove, Myndi marveled at the guardrails constructed by the WPA workers from heavy rock and mortar barrier along the entire length of the Scenic Highway. She was amazed the low walls were still in such excellent condition.

"My Grandfather helped construct these barriers." Myndi said to Ginger.

Myndi and Ginger arrived at Multnomah Falls earlier than anticipated. They took a leisurely walk up the path to the bridge over the pool of water that formed at the base of the falls, before the water began its second fall. Their walk was exhilarating with beautiful ferns, wild trilliums, and moss-covered areas along the sides of the path. Ginger didn't mind her leash as she led Myndi. The spray from the waterfall, when they paused on the bridge, was refreshing as Myndi gazed up to the originating point where the water cascaded over the ledge. It was breathtaking as it careened down and under the bridge where she and Ginger stood. After picture taking, she walked Ginger back to the car and then over to the lodge. She purchased a postcard in the gift store to send to her grandmother. As she sat in the restaurant, adjacent to the gift shop, sipping a cup of coffee, she wrote a short note about what she'd seen so far that morning and how much she was enjoying her Honda.

"Save the postcards, Grandma," she added to the note. "They will make good visuals for my classes when I begin to teach."

The caption under the picture on the postcard noted:

> *The water drops 620 feet from its origin on Larch Mountain. It is the second highest year-round waterfall in the nation. The Lodge is a stone structure, built in 1925 by A. E. Doyle.*

When Myndi's returned to the car, she checked her itinerary and spoke to her navigation system to determine the distance to the town of Umatilla, where she had decided to spend the night. She chuckled to herself as the metallic computer voice came back,

"The distance to Umatilla, Oregon from Multnomah Falls is 120 miles on Interstate-84. Estimated travel time is two hours and fifteen minutes."

Myndi had been reading about some of the places she would travel through and the city of Umatilla seemed as if it would be fascinating regarding its geography and history. She'd read how Lewis & Clark first visited the area in April 1806 as they surveyed the Pacific Northwest for the U.S. Government. She knew there would be a lot of history there, after she found a place to spend the night. She planned to explore the Umatilla visitor's center, library, museum, and historical sites around the area, if there was time.

When Myndi and Ginger arrived in Umatilla, the sight of a beautiful old hotel intrigued Myndi. In the lobby, she picked up brochures that explained the old building was once a flourmill. Remodeled recently, the exterior and interior decor was styled in the tradition of an elegant 18th century European chalet.

The hotel amenities included a swimming pool, sauna, and fitness room. The rooms had all been upgraded with cable television, queen-size beds with lovely English coverlets, and matching curtains at the windows. A computer with Internet access was located in the lobby. *I'll email Jeff about today's travels and tell him how much I'm already missing him,* she thought as she gave the clerk her information for the overnight stay.

That night, Myndi wrote the first entry in her travel journal:

Myndi's Journal:

Tuesday—June 15

My goodness, Jeff and Grandma, my head is spinning with all the history I've already encountered in just one day. I'm having so much fun. Ginger is enjoying her spot on the back window ledge too. Several people have commented during our stops about how cute she looks lying there. She's good company for me, and I get to stretch my legs too, whenever she needs to get out to romp.

Grandma, I'm so glad we planned for me to travel the old Historic Columbia River Highway on the way to Multnomah Falls. The smaller Horsetail and Bridal Veil Falls were beautiful and the majestic views of the Columbia River were breathtaking from the higher elevations, especially at Crown Point. When we arrived at Multnomah Falls and walked up the pathway to the bridge over the lower part of the falls, the ferns and trilliums were so pretty. The spray from the falls cooled us as we stood on the bridge. The old historic lodge was a beautiful stone structure (I took Ginger back to the car while I explored the interior).

From Multnomah Falls, we got on Interstate 84, and made stops in Hood River and The Dalles. I gathered literature all along the way. It'll be fun sharing it with my students. I had already picked up some brochures from Vista House at the Crown Point gift shop and at Multnomah Falls. While in The Dalles, I acquired a large cardboard box for my "souvenir" collections.

We arrived in Umatilla about 2 o'clock and I found a quaint little room in an old hotel in the center of town. After depositing my luggage in the room, Ginger and I headed out to explore this city that provided us with many vantage points for *viewing Mt. Hood and Mt. Adams in the distance. I found even more brochures in the library with pictures of the Umatilla River as it empties into the Columbia River, and of the McNary Dam dedicated by President Dwight D. Eisenhower on September 23, 1954.*

The Jacuzzi hot tub in my room was so relaxing tonight. However, that may have had something to do with the delightful glass of Riesling wine I had while soaking!

I look forward to the trip to Kellogg, Idaho, tomorrow and to renewing my friendship with Paula as I help her with the preparations for her wedding on Friday. Paula has a fun personality and she's always full of surprises!

Chapter Three:

Kellogg, Idaho

It was 8 o'clock the next morning by the time Myndi had showered, loaded her overnight luggage into the car, and taken Ginger for a short walk. The hotel breakfast room was open but, because her evening meal in the hotel dining room had been a bowl of their famous minestrone soup with a side order of homemade garlic bread, she wasn't hungry for a large breakfast. She settled for an apple muffin and a cup of coffee and, from the counter, took an apple and a banana for snacks along the way. After checking out of the hotel, she mailed her grandmother a postcard depicting the Umatilla River and McNary Dam. She saw to it that Ginger was comfortable on her blanket, and then she headed for Interstate 82.

The car navigator declared, "The mileage to Kellogg, Idaho, from Umatilla, Oregon, is 240 miles."

Myndi chuckled at the sight of Ginger in the rearview mirror cocking her head to the sound of the strange voice.

Her thoughts turned to Paula. They had been close friends for three of their four years at college. Myndi's first roommate, chosen by the college, seemed okay in the beginning. They had met for a cup of tea before the college term began and were excited to be moving in together, but into their fourth week, Myndi found their personalities and study habits differed too greatly to be compatible roommates. It was taking a toll on her studies.

Myndi met Paula in their Beginning German class, and when Paula said a room was available in the off-campus boarding house where she lived, Myndi made an appointment to see it that afternoon. Paula took Myndi to meet Mrs. Jansen, the owner, and Myndi moved in that Saturday.

During their senior year, Paula transferred to a college nearer to her home and graduated in

December. Paula wrote to Myndi in January and said she and Scott had gotten engaged and that their pending marriage would be in June. She asked Myndi to be her Maid of Honor. In her letter, Paula said it would be a candlelight wedding on the night of Friday, June 18.

Myndi planned to arrive in Kellogg in the early afternoon so that she would have the evening and all the next day to visit with Paula, rekindle her friendship with Paula's parents, and see Scott again, who she'd also met in college. Paula and Scott, and Jeff and Myndi had double-dated on a couple of occasions.

Twenty minutes later, Myndi exited onto Highway 395. At a rest stop seventy miles from Spokane, she saw a sign advertising:

SMOOTHIES—BLUEBERRY MILKSHAKES
STRAWBERRY SHORT CAKE
1-MILE AHEAD—ON YOUR RIGHT

She had seen men, women, and children working in the fields for the past several miles. It reminded her of her own childhood, when she, too, worked in the bean, raspberry, and strawberry fields during summer vacations. Her fondest memories were of the strawberry patches. She recalled her red-stained fingers, the smell of the fresh strawberries, and the delicious taste of the berries that never made it into the box.

She pulled into the fruit stand parking lot and was amazed at the variety of fresh berries and vegetables, and the jars of jams and jellies lining the shelves. She picked a few items to take to Paula's parents and ordered a Fresh Strawberry Milkshake to go. Back on the road, she took the next exit onto Interstate 90, which would take her the remaining 130 miles into the city of Kellogg.

The fresh, plump, berry pieces were too large to suck through the straw, but each sip as she drove down the highway added a delicious coating on her tongue.

The drive through the Spokane Valley was lush and green. Agricultural products were growing on farms throughout the valley. Myndi remembered that her grandfather had told her his brother, her great uncle, Bernard, and great aunt, Irene, had once lived here, in the Spokane area. They owned their own antique furniture store, but after retirement, they moved to Seattle, Washington, to be near their daughter and her family. As pretty and serene as this valley was, Myndi could not help but wonder how they must have missed living here.

It was 2 o'clock when Myndi pulled up to the home of Paula and her family. The house was an attractive two-story Cape Cod-style structure, just as beautiful as Myndi remembered it from two years ago when she'd spent a week of summer vacation with Paula. Paula had shown Myndi around her hometown and the surrounding Kellogg area during that week.

History, of course, was one of Myndi's favorite subjects throughout her school years, and on her previous visit to Kellogg, she had jotted down some of what she called "neat facts." These were:

The Kellogg area was called "Silver Valley"

because the first silver strike had been made in 1885. The Kellogg Bunker Hill Mine and Smelter Company were located here for approximately 100 years. And Kellogg was known worldwide as a leader in silver mining. But thousands of people were suddenly left without a job when the company was forced to close because the silver vein had run its course.

There are many old prospectors' stories and legends about the area, and how the silver was first found. Many of the abandoned mineshafts were sought out by tourists and photographers.

When the mine closed down, the townspeople held a brainstorming meeting and came up with the idea of a snow skiing area and the Alpine theme was adopted. They built a gondola that rose to the top of the mountain formerly called Jackass Ski Bowl, and which they quickly renamed Silver Mountain. In their efforts to change their image, they also renamed Jackass Gulch to Jacob's Gulch. Myndi loved the view from the top of Silver Mountain, but she was especially fond of the beautiful Coeur d'Alene River and enjoyed driving across the numerous bridges that crisscrossed the river as she traveled along the highway.

Paula had been watching for Myndi from the swing on the front porch and came running to greet her. She'd been helping her mother prepare a variety of Mexican dishes all morning in anticipation of the get-together scheduled for early evening.

"Oh, Paula, you look so domestic in that apron," Myndi laughed as she gave Paula a hug and kiss.

"Oh, I know," laughed Paula. "Mom says I'm in training. Anyway, Myndi, the get-together tonight is a welcome/get acquainted with Myndi gathering, just for you, so you can meet Scott's and my friends and the other wedding attendants."

They went inside. "This is your room, Myndi. Hope you like it. I freshened everything yesterday for you."

"It's lovely, Paula."

While hanging up her clothes, Myndi told Paula about Jeff's marriage proposal on the evening before her graduation.

"Oh, Myndi," Paula squealed. "That is so exciting!" And she squealed again when Myndi showed off her engagement ring.

"Now that you're unpacked," Paula smiled, "why don't you grab a quick shower and maybe a little nap before this evening? I'll just keep helping Mom."

"Sounds great, Paula, but first I have to go down and say hello to your mom."

"Dear, Myndi," said Paula's mom. "I'm almost finished here in the kitchen, but thank you for offering to help. We're so glad you came, and Paula couldn't be happier. I think Paula had a wonderful idea about you taking a shower and nap. You must be tired from your drive. See you soon, honey. We'll catch up later. Okay?"

"Okay. I'm off to freshen up." Myndi waved a hand over her shoulder as she climbed the stairs.

The guest bedroom was fresh and airy. It had a canopy bed with a silk chiffon covering over the top, and matching curtains on the windows that looked out at Silver Mountain. The coverlet on the bed was a filet-crochet, handmade by Paula's mother. A cute little dog bed had been placed in one corner of the room for Ginger, and the dog quickly snuggled into the padded cushion.

It had been a long drive from Umatilla to Kellogg, so Myndi was grateful for the shower and a brief nap. Afterwards, she helped Paula and her mother with the final preparations before the party,

The evening had a "South of the Border" theme, with Spanish decorations, music, and specialty foods, and of course, plenty of ice-cold margaritas to drink.

Myndi's Journal:

> *Wednesday—June 16*
>
> *I was glad I had picked up, written, and mailed the postcard of the picturesque Coeur d'Alene River to Grandma before I arrived in Kellogg. It was a long drive for me from Umatilla to Paula's house. Ginger and I didn't make many stops along the way, however I did stop at one of the many farm-stands along the highway and enjoyed a delicious fresh strawberry milkshake. I also picked up some fresh vegetables, "Mama Sophie's" homemade peanut brittle that Paula and I used to enjoy anytime we could get it while in college, and a couple jars of jam for Paula's parents. I loved the drive through the Spokane Valley. The farmland looked incredibly fertile, and the Coeur d'Alene River, which I crossed many times, was amazingly picturesque. I saw several campsites and walking paths.*

It was fun reconnecting with Paula and her family, and it was so sweet of them to have planned the surprise "South of the Border" fiesta for me so I could meet their friends. I helped with the cleanup after everyone left and then we said our goodnights. Ginger had already trundled off to our room and I found her sleeping snug on her dog blanket when I came into the bedroom.

I'm sure happy and excited about being here for Paula.

Tomorrow is going to be another big day for all of us!

Thursday—June 17

What a busy day today! It began with the early morning fitting for my dress. Paula had already picked out the gown she wants me to wear as her Maid of Honor. It is a lovely turquoise princess-style with spaghetti straps over the shoulders. I felt so pretty in it and thought it went well with my hair color.—Can't wait to see the pictures!

At noon, a friend of Paula's threw her a bridal shower. The theme was "lingerie," and Paula couldn't help but blush when she opened the boxes of sexy negligees. Everyone laughed when she said the items would definitely be packed with her trousseau. After the shower, we headed for the church for the wedding rehearsal.

Two trial rehearsals were made before everyone agreed that things would most likely go smoothly the next day. Extra time was taken with Paula's six-year-old niece and four-year-old nephew, who are the flower girl and ring-bearer. The rehearsal dinner afterward was held at an Italian restaurant. A strolling violin ensemble played music all during the meal.

I was comfortable in the company of Paula's friends and family. Grandma, your postcard for today ended up being a picture of Paula and Scott, and me, which we took with my cell phone and forwarded to Jeff. I hope you both like it!

At the wedding rehearsal dinner, Myndi was seated across the table from Jason, Scott's best man. She couldn't help noticing how handsome he was with his blond hair, deep blue eyes, and captivating smile. The forest green turtleneck sweater he wore gave his blue eyes a greenish tint.

Myndi looked up from her plate several times, and on one occasion, she blushed when Jason winked at her, not so much because of the wink, but because he'd caught her looking at him. She wondered, as she lowered her eyes, if he could read her thoughts.

After dinner, during the evening dancing, Jason cut in on several of the other young men in the group when they danced with her, and before long others didn't even bother to ask.

Myndi omitted these thoughts and the attraction she was feeling for Jason from her journal.

Myndi awoke happy to see sunshine flooding her room on her friend's wedding day. Paula was busy with last-minute packing, final wedding and reception arrangements, and numerous other last minute preparations, so Myndi stayed out of her way. She was glad when Paula's mother said she had a telephone call.

Myndi rushed to the phone to talk with Jeff. He was probably calling to get an update on her adventure so far. But Myndi was surprised to find Jason on the phone, and even more surprised when he invited her out for a day of sightseeing and lunch at a restaurant in Coeur d'Alene, a nearby city. Myndi was glad for the diversion and accepted immediately. She noticed the raised eyebrow Paula exhibited as she left with Jason a few minutes later. Since the day was so warm, so she left Ginger at home with Paula.

Jason headed down the road driving his "classic" 1955 yellow Cadillac convertible. With the top down and the beautiful sunny day, Myndi understood the reason for Jason's suntanned features. She felt as though she had known Jason much longer than just since the previous evening. On the way to Coeur d'Alene, they talked about their childhoods and the plans they each had for their futures.

Coeur d'Alene was a forty-minute drive from Paula's home, so Jason took a couple of short side trips through the beautiful green valley. They then drove the route along the Coeur d'Alene Lake before stopping for lunch. The restaurant was located at the water's edge and large picture windows overlooked the beautiful deep blue lake. People were enjoying all sorts of water toys out there: ski-doos, water skiing, canoeing, sailboats, as well as splashing in several swimming areas. They watched from their table as three rowboats with six people per boat competed in some kind of race.

The restaurant menu had a variety of sandwiches, so Jason suggested that they order a different kind and then split their orders so they could each sample two kinds.

After lunch, they walked down a path to the lake and watched the water skiers before realizing they had better head back to Kellogg to prepare for the wedding.

Jason and Myndi arrived back at Paula's house at 3 o'clock. After Jason left, Paula was full of questions about their day—how Myndi and Jason got along, where they had lunch, and what they ate. Myndi explained how nice Jason was to be with, spoke of his great smile, and how, with the top down on his Caddy, her ponytail flipped back and forth in the breeze.

"Glad you had a nice time, Myndi." Paula whispered, shrugging her shoulders.

The candlelight wedding ceremony was beautiful and, as Myndi preceded Paula down the aisle, she felt compelled to focus on Jason, who was standing next to Scott at the altar. Jason's smile was captivating. She hoped her smile did not reveal too much.

Paula was a beautiful bride, and the ceremony went just as she and Scott had planned. Everyone laughed when Paula's niece and nephew skipped instead of walked down the aisle and they stopped to say hi to people all along the way. And, of course, the two children couldn't stand still during the ceremony—they shifted from one foot to the other and waved to their parents. The reception included a finger-food buffet. Laughter continually erupted during the photo sessions. Several friends and family toasted the bride and groom and then, after they cut the cake and shared their piece, and made a toast to each other, the new bride and groom were ready to leave on their honeymoon.

Myndi helped Paula change from her wedding dress into a light green two-piece outfit, with matching shoes and a frilly summer hat. Then they said their goodbyes. It was Myndi who caught Paula's bouquet.

Paula and Scott had arranged with a disc jockey to play dance music after their departure, so many of the wedding guests stayed late. Myndi and Jason danced together the entire evening and Myndi felt butterflies in her stomach when Jason lightly brushed her cheek with a kiss.

Myndi's Journal for Friday, June 18 took some thought. She knew people would be reading her entries, so she purposely left out the part about Jason, and focused entirely on Paula's wedding.

How beautiful she was as a bride, and how wonderful was the candlelit wedding ceremony. She expressed how great it was to be a part of her friend's wedding. She wrote of the dress Paula purchased for her. Myndi ended her journal, "I'm so looking forward to our trip tomorrow."

Myndi was happily exhausted by the time she finally finished her journal entry. She turned off the light and went to sleep. Tomorrow would be a day on the road, as she and Ginger headed to the next stop on their adventure: Yellowstone Park in Montana.

Early Saturday morning, Myndi loaded her luggage into the car. Ginger was already curled up on her window ledge when Myndi's cell phone rang. It was Jason.

"Hi, Myndi. You're probably ready to head out, but I got wondering if you'd like to stop by my place as you head out of town. I'd like to fix you an early breakfast. I'd like to show you my place."

"I'm packed and ready to leave now," Myndi replied. "But I only had a cup of coffee with Paula's parents as they finished their breakfast, so your offer sounds like fun. Give me your address and directions."

"You can't get lost, Myndi. My place sits about fifty feet off the highway."

Fifteen minutes later, Myndi pulled up in front of Jason's home. He was waiting for her on the porch, sipping a cup of coffee. He welcomed Ginger and Myndi inside.

"Breakfast is all prepared. It didn't take long after you agreed to come, Myndi. I've set up the table on the back patio deck. It's such a delightful warm morning," Jason said as he led her to a chair by the table.

After they'd finished the meal, Myndi grinned and said, "You did well, Jason." She patted her napkin to her lips.

"Thanks, Myndi. I've been living as a bachelor all these years. It's been fun cooking and learning new recipes, but how can you go wrong with bacon, eggs, and toast for breakfast?" He paused, and then asked sheepishly, "Myndi? Are you in a real hurry today? Can you stay and spend the day and evening with me? I had a wonderful time yesterday at lunch on the river and again last night as we danced. I don't believe in the old cliché of love-at-first-sight, but I'm more attracted to you than any other woman I've dated. But, I'll understand if you have to move on."

"I'm flattered, Jason, and I have to confess that I also enjoyed our time together yesterday. Yeah, I can stay—for a while anyway," she nodded, ignoring the inner voice telling her to reject the invitation.

"I'll go out to the car and get my copy of our itinerary, Jason. You probably know a lot about the areas I plan to visit. Perhaps you can suggest some additional sites along the way?"

"Super, Myndi. I'll just throw the dishes in the dishwasher while you get your paperwork and we can scan them over another cup of coffee. Okay?"

"Hey, your itinerary looks super, Myndi. These are all great places to visit," Jason said after glancing through Myndi's route. Then he exclaimed, "Wow! I can't believe we've been sitting here for over an hour. I sure didn't mean to bore you with all my history, Myndi." he apologized.

"It's okay, Jason. I've learned that you're 28 years old. You've been a real estate salesman since your graduation from college, and in the spring of 2002, you purchased an office in town. You have three realtors working for you. But you handle most of your real estate dealings from your home office."

She laughed when Jason chuckled. "Right on, Myndi!"

"Well, it was only fair, Jason. You had to listen to me go on about my childhood for fifteen minutes!"

"But, I'm not done yet, Myndi. There's more. I have my own Internet website. I love the real estate profession, and I'm licensed not only in Idaho, but also in Washington and Montana. Oh, no! Now I'm boring you. I saw that yawn."

"No, I'm not bored, Jason. But I do think it's time for me to be on my way."

"Myndi, I'd like to give you a chance to really get to know me, and me to know you. Perhaps see where our relationship could go? Would you stay for dinner? I've got two steaks marinating in the fridge."

"Now I know I was right when I saw a certain expression on your face as you asked. Yes! I'll stay a while longer."

The afternoon passed quickly as Myndi and Jason revealed more of their past lives and future goals. Jason's college major was computer science/engineering, and he enjoyed helping the local high school students solve computer problems. Once a week, he taught a computer class at night at the community college, designated especially for senior citizens. Myndi learned Jason was also an only child. His father had died of cancer in 1995, and his mother passed away in 1999. It was apparent from the sad expression that came over his face, replacing his natural gleaming eyes and smile, that he missed his parents terribly.

Then, taking Myndi's hand, he led her to the living room where he got out a Memory Photo Book of his parents and himself that he'd put together. Myndi saw the resemblances between Jason and his father in their similar facial features. She especially liked the pictures of Jason as a young child.

Myndi told Jason all about Jeff and their early childhood and their planned wedding next June.

"Wow!" Jason interrupted, as he took Myndi's hand again and walked her into the kitchen." I didn't realize it was so late. Let's get some dinner, okay?"

"Great. It's been a while since breakfast," Myndi grinned while squeezing Jason's hand in return. "All that talking has made me hungry."

"I'll put the steaks on the backyard barbeque and foil-wrap some spuds. Myndi, do you want to prepare a tossed green salad to go along with it?"

"Sure, Jason! You go ahead. I think I can find everything in your fridge."

The evening air cooled when the afternoon sun faded, aided by the breeze off the Silver Mountain ski slopes. Jason built a crackling fire in the living room fireplace, and set a lovely candle-lit table in the adjacent dining room. He'd picked a bouquet of flowers while the steaks were browning, and when he returned to the kitchen he popped open a bottle of rosé wine and served it as they began their dinner. When they finished eating, Jason took the remaining wine to drink in front of the fireplace.

Myndi knew even before Jason asked that she would spend the night curled up in bed beside him. She knew it wasn't the wine that had gone to her head, and she knew she shouldn't do it, but the longing she felt for Jason's arms overcame logic.

The two of them woke several times during the night. Their lovemaking was all that Myndi had imagined. Jason was tender and sweet and the thrill Myndi felt at the height of each new lovemaking session was more wonderful than the last.

CHAPTER FOUR:

YELLOWSTONE PARK

MYNDI WOKE ON SUNDAY MORNING to the aroma of fresh-brewed coffee, which Jason brought to her as she stretched herself awake.

"I don't want you to leave, Myndi. I hope you don't think last night was just a one-night-stand for me. I think I'm falling in love with you."

"I know, Jason. But I'm really confused. I never should have let last night happen. I love Jeff. My future is planned with Jeff. I have a teaching job that starts in September. And I need to be there for Grandma Kate. Everything I've ever known is in the Tri-Mountains area of Oregon. But, Jason," she blurted, "I having strong feelings for you, too!"

"Shhh. Don't say anything right now Myn...."

"Jason, I have to," she interrupted. "I'm so mixed

up. Everything is happening so fast. I can't stay here with you! I have so many people to consider and all my life I've programmed myself to please others!" Myndi sobbed uncontrollably.

Jason touched her hand and then left the room.

"I prepared breakfast while you showered, Myndi," Jason said when she entered the kitchen.

"Just another cup of coffee, Jason. I need to get going on my trip."

"But, Myndi," Jason said while she sipped the coffee, "There's a three-day real estate seminar I need to attend Monday through Wednesday, June 28 through June 30. I know your itinerary didn't include it, but maybe you could alter it a little bit and meet me on Sunday, June 27? Before the seminar begins. We could spend some time together in Steamboat Springs, Colorado."

"Steamboat Springs!" Myndi said, then shivered. "No! I'm not going to Steamboat Springs, Jason." She put her empty coffee cup on the counter, picked up her overnight bag, and headed for the door. Ginger following close behind her.

"I'm sorry, Myndi." Jason said as he opened the car door and let Ginger in, and then brushed a quick kiss gently across Myndi's cheek.

"Goodbye, Jason," Myndi murmured.

Through her tears, she saw Jason waving when she glanced at the rearview mirror as she drove away.

Shortly after leaving Kellogg, and very near the border with Montana, the time zone changed from Pacific Daylight Savings to Mountain Time. Myndi had lost an hour of travel time. The drive was beautiful, but lonely, as she made her way east along Highway 90.

She pulled the car off the road at a viewpoint and allowed herself to cry uncontrollably. The moment the car stopped, Ginger jumped down from her window ledge and was in Myndi's lap, licking away the tears streaming down her owner's face. Myndi sat stroking Ginger's fur, hugging her close, knowing that Ginger sensed something was wrong. Myndi's thoughts turned to Jeff.

Jeff had come into her life when she was a sixth-grader at Bradley Grade School. They grew up in the same neighborhood, but he attended parochial school and was in the seventh grade. As children, they often hung out with neighborhood kids. Winter months were especially fun when there was enough snow to go sledding or build forts and have snowball fights. Summer months found them playing games outdoors, like tag and hide-and-seek.

All year round, the neighborhood kids would also get together at one of their houses to watch cartoons, *Captain Kangaroo*, and the various local shows broadcast from Portland. Those times together almost always included popcorn and soft drinks. On a couple of occasions, their parents took them to Portland so they could participate in the audience while watching the live taping of the local cartoon shows.

She recalled being a school crossing guard in grade school, which required her to be on duty early every morning. Her mind traveled back to the morning in the seventh grade when Jeff stopped at her corner on his way to school. He handed her a fresh velvety red rose, and from then on, it seemed there was no one else for either of them.

Her eyes brimmed with tears again as the guilt of the last two days encompassed her. When she felt cried out, she attempted to regain her composure. A few minutes later, she and Ginger continued on their way.

Several miles up the road, at another viewpoint, Myndi and Ginger walked to the edge of the guardrail. Myndi took several deep breaths in the early morning breeze and gazed out across the wide expanse of the Montana hills in the distance, and at the forested area below. She did a few stretching exercises and then let Ginger explore while she took a photograph of the scenery. She felt the need to review her memories of Jeff, but she was having a hard time dealing with how guilty she felt about cheating on him.

Two hours later, Myndi pulled off the highway again. This time they were at a rest stop. She and Ginger walked past a picnic site and down a pathway toward a small crystal-clear running creek. A splash of cold water on her face felt so refreshing. Ginger seemed to enjoy the run and exploration of the wooded area.

"Ginger! Come on, little girl." Myndi smiled as Ginger approached. "We can continue now. I feel so much better and I can't wait to see what lies ahead."

At noon, Myndi pulled into a restaurant parking lot in Missoula, Montana. The restaurant was crowded with local patrons and a few tourists. It felt good just listening to the light chatter and laughter coming from the counter area. The waitress asked where she was from, and Myndi said Tri-Mountains, a suburb of Portland, Oregon.

No one outside the area has ever heard of Tri-Mountains and Myndi loved explaining the origin of her hometown's name. Mount Hood, Mount Saint Helens, and Mount Rainier are visible from almost everywhere in town. It felt good to talk with someone about home.

While paying her check, Myndi asked a couple sitting at the counter if they knew how long it would take to drive to Livingston, her next stop. They said Highway 90 is in good shape after recent roadwork, that it was roughly 220-miles, and would probably take her three and a half hours.

Before Myndi left the parking lot, she called Grandma Kate using her cell phone and reported that she was going to spend the night in Livingston, Montana, and that she had set up a tour of Yellowstone for the morning. Grandma Kate said she was glad Myndi was having such a good time and that she was really enjoying the postcards.

Her grandmother also mentioned a brother of Grandfather Frank who had lived in Livingston. He had been a sheriff in Yellowstone Park, and he and his wife owned a flower nursery and greenhouse that supplied fresh flowers to florists. Kate said Myndi's great-uncle John had died of cancer several years before her grandfather's death.

"I love you, Grandma," Myndi said, and thanked her again for her graduation presents. Myndi wasn't quite ready to talk with Jeff, so she told Kate to tell him she loved him, too. She hoped her grandmother hadn't detected the confusion she was feeling.

Myndi then made her way down the highway toward Livingston, arriving in town at 3:45 p.m. She went directly to the library to research her great-uncle John. She was happy to find that he appeared to have had an eventful life. He had been a sheriff; had won awards for being a No. 1 Chef at several restaurants, and owned the flower nursery with his wife. At one time, he had run for mayor.

The librarian told her that the city of Gardiner, just a short drive down US 89, was only one mile from the North Entrance of Yellowstone Park. After a snack stop for Ginger, they headed for Gardiner.

Myndi found a nice Comfort Inn motel that accepted pets and checked herself and Ginger in for the night. She also made arrangements for a guided tour of the park for the next morning. The desk clerk convinced her that a guided tour was really the best way to see Yellowstone because she wouldn't have to drive, and because the guides know the best spots for viewing bear, buffalo, and other animals, as well as Old Faithful and other geysers. Myndi made her reservation for 7 o'clock in the morning and asked the desk clerk for a 5 o'clock wakeup call. Myndi thanked the desk clerk for her offer to watch Ginger while she was gone.

Her room was very clean and neat with a beautiful mountain view. The amenities of the motel included three hot tubs available to the patrons, and a free continental breakfast in the morning. She made two entries in her journal that evening.

Saturday—June 19

I spent another day and evening in Kellogg, Idaho. Ginger and I left early this morning for Yellowstone Park.

Sunday—June 20

The trip today was a long one for me, lonely at times. I kept recalling memories of home, but I certainly was enjoying the scenery, the people I met, and the research on my Great-Uncle John I did at the Livingston library. In some places, Montana looks very much like the forested areas in Oregon. I enjoyed my breakfast in Missoula and the laughter and chatter of the locals at the breakfast counter. My waitress was especially gracious and we had a good talk. I am exhausted as I write this tonight, but I am so looking forward to Yellowstone Park tomorrow.

Myndi's wakeup call came at 5 a.m. sharp. Bounding out of bed, she hurriedly showered, pulled her hair back into a ponytail, and skipped down the stairs, taking Ginger for her morning walk. Myndi had just enough time to eat a light continental breakfast before leaving Ginger with the desk clerk. At 7 o'clock, Henry, the guide, pulled up to the front of the motel in a small bus, which seated sixteen people. Nine people had signed up for the tour, but Henry said he had to make another stop to pick up an additional six people from another motel.

Less than an hour into the tour, Myndi knew she'd made the right decision. Henry told stories and recounted the history of the park. Yellowstone was America's first National Park, established in 1872 when Ulysses S. Grant was President. The park straddles three states: Wyoming, Montana, and Idaho.

A gasp could be heard throughout the bus when Henry made the astounding announcement that the park contained 2,219,823 acres, which is more than the states of Delaware and Rhode Island combined.

It is home to a large variety of wildlife, including grizzly bears, wolves, buffalo (bison), and elk. Henry also explained how Old Faithful, and the park's other extraordinary geysers and hot springs, are preserved within the park's boundaries. Henry was knowledgeable and enthusiastic.

It was clear to everyone on the bus that Henry loved his job, but they all stood corrected when he stated this was not a job—"Every morning, when I get up, I am on vacation."

There were a few young school children and several couples on the tour, and Myndi could not help but feel that it would have been nice to be able to share this experience with Jeff—or Jason.

The tour took longer than Myndi anticipated, but luckily, Henry had not rushed them through it.

She made arrangements to spend another night at the motel to catch up on sleep. She was beginning to feel better, and looking forward to the rest of her trip.

She retrieved Ginger, fed her dinner, and then they went for a walk around the grounds of the

Comfort Inn. She snapped some photos of the surrounding mountains and then took Ginger to the room while she went to the nearby restaurant for a light supper. Then she treated herself to a really nice soak in one of the motel's hot tubs.

The drive tomorrow would be long. She hoped to make it all the way across Montana, travel a short way through the northeast corner of Wyoming, and arrive in Keystone, South Dakota, to visit Mt. Rushmore and Crazy Horse Monument. At 8 o'clock, she climbed into bed and proceeded to fall sound asleep after making an entry in her journal.

Myndi's Journal:

> *Monday—June 21*
>
> *The beauty and splendor of what I have seen so far, especially on the guided tour through Yellowstone Park today, is more than I could ever imagine. I would not have seen, nor been so well informed about the park, its animals, and its history if I had just driven through on my own*
>
> *Besides, it was so much fun talking with other tourists—where they had been, what they had done, and where they were going. The tour bus made several stops along the way for picture taking and I even took a few photos through the window of grizzly bears, buffalo, birds, and wildflowers.*
>
> *For Grandma's postcard today, I purchased a string of photos at the Yellowstone gift shop, and while we were stopped for lunch, I addressed, stamped, and mailed the packet to Grandma so it*

will have the Yellowstone Park postmark and commemorative stamp.

We arrived back at the motel around 4 o'clock and I was surprised when Henry, our tour guide, gave me a stack of flyers and National Park information to use in my sixth grade class. I had mentioned my recent college graduation and forthcoming teaching job to Henry when we stopped at a rest area.

CHAPTER FIVE:

KEYSTONE, SOUTH DAKOTA, MT. RUSHMORE, & CHIEF CRAZY HORSE MONUMENT

AFTER MYNDI'S CONTINENTAL BREAKFAST and table scraps for Ginger, they went for a short walk and then continued on their way to South Dakota. Since it would be such a long driving day, she asked the restaurant to prepare a sandwich, chips, an apple, and a banana sack lunch, so she would not have to stop at a restaurant along the way. They drove back up State Highway 89 to Livingston, and got back on Highway 90.

Highway 90 would take them all the way across Montana to the town of Hardin, where it would drop down into Wyoming and continue on to the town Gillette. At Gillette, she would exit onto

Highway 16 and take that road to where it met up with Highway 385. If everything worked out according to plan, Highway 385 would bring them into Keystone, South Dakota. According to her car navigator system, they would be traveling 590 miles today. Given time for rest stops and an average cruising speed of 60 to 70 miles per hour, Myndi figured the trip would take a little over nine hours.

Myndi made it as far as the outskirts of Gillette, Wyoming, before she was too tired to push on. They had traveled more than 500 miles and had been on the road seven hours. She and Ginger both needed to rest. A signboard advertising a Comfort Inn Motel beckoned. She had been satisfied with the cleanliness and relaxing atmosphere of the motel chain's Livingston location, so she requested the Inn's telephone number from her navigation system. At the next rest stop, Myndi called and reserved a room. She and Ginger were both happy to get out of the car. After a light dinner, they took a walk around town and found a school playground where Ginger explored and Myndi swung on a swing.

Myndi's Journal:

Tuesday—June 22

This was a long travel day for us. Again, I enjoyed the beauty of the scenery and wildlife (coyotes, antelope, lots of jackrabbits, and even a herd of ten buffalo). I pulled over to the side of the road once to watch a soaring eagle against the azure-blue sky. The eagle's call was so loud—a long screech. It was breathtaking to watch the eagle catch a wind current and float motionless for a while before starting a swooping decline into the forest below, and out of my sight. Ginger and I are really tired tonight. She is already curled up on her fleece blanket in the corner and snoring lightly. I'm sure looking forward to Mt. Rushmore and viewing the Chief Crazy Horse Monument tomorrow.

Myndi passed on her continental breakfast Wednesday morning, opting instead for a poached egg on toast, a slice of ham, and a bowl of peaches ordered in the adjoining restaurant. She took Ginger for their early morning walk, and then returned to their room. She placed a long overdue call to Jeff.

Myndi had text-messaged Jeff from her cell phone several times during the trip, telling him what a great time she was having and that she loved him. But she had not actually conversed with him since leaving Tri-Mountain. It was still early in the day, before he had to leave for work. She needed—and wanted—to know how he was doing.

Jeff said he was glad she called when she did; he was just on his way out the door. She told him how she missed him and that she regretted he was not with her on the trip. She did mention what a really fun time she was having. He said he loved and missed her, too. He said he was learning so much about the legal profession from his mentors, and even from that limited exposure, he knew he would enjoy becoming a lawyer.

Jeff also said he had dropped in on Grandma Kate several times to see how she was doing, and Kate had filled him in on Myndi's trip with all the news from the postcards and phone calls. He was so glad she was having a good time. They closed their conversation with love. Myndi had made up her mind that she would wait until she returned home to tell him about Jason and the time they had spent together. There was no need to go into it over the telephone.

By 9:30, Myndi was ready to depart. Ginger jumped onto her window ledge when Myndi loaded their overnight bags. Myndi estimated that it was about 90 miles to Keystone, South Dakota. She was thankful that she had made the decision to stop for the night. The break from driving refreshed her mind and body, but she knew she still had some soul searching to do.

It was 11:30 when they arrived in Keystone. Myndi went directly into the Chamber of Commerce to pick up information on Mt. Rushmore and Chief Crazy Horse Monument.

The park and the monument attractions were located in the Black Hills area of South Dakota, within a two-mile radius of Keystone, so Myndi decided to explore those tours on her own. She learned at the Chamber of Commerce that dogs were not allowed at Mt. Rushmore, except for two pet areas near the parking lot. She could have rented a kennel for Ginger, but the day was cool, so with the car windows partially down, Ginger would patiently wait there for her master.

The entrance to the Mount Rushmore site was draped on both sides with flags from every state in the USA. Myndi learned that the Memorial was America's Shrine of Democracy. The four presidents whose faces are carved in the granite mountainside are George Washington, Thomas Jefferson, Theodore Roosevelt, and Abraham Lincoln. From the viewing deck on the top floor of the library building, Myndi was awestruck by the size of the four faces and the artistic craft it took to carve them in granite. She took a walking path at the base of the mountain and stopped to read a plaque along the route. The quote by Gerard Baker, the park superintendent, gave her goose bumps. She read:

> *Mount Rushmore is a memorial that symbolizes America, and Americans should never lose sight of their cultural beginnings.*

She returned to the car laden with brochures and some video discs. Ginger was happy to get out of the car and stroll with Myndi along her very own walking path, away from all the tourists.

Myndi was awestruck again when she arrived at the Chief Crazy Horse Monument, located just a few miles away from Mt. Rushmore. It was also a carved structure on the side of a granite mountain. An informative flyer stated:

> *Crazy Horse Memorial monument is under construction in the Black Hills of South Dakota. It is of Crazy Horse, an Oglala Lakota warrior, riding a horse and pointing into the distance. When the carving is completed, it will be 641 feet*

long and 563 feet high. Chief Crazy Horse's head is complete and is 87 feet 6 inches high. The horse's head will be 219 feet tall—22 stories high when finished.

A plaque denoted the commemoration of the Chief Crazy Horse Monument by South Dakota's senators. Additional promotional material that Myndi picked up for her class stated:

Korczak Ziolkowski (1908-1982), a sculptor, was invited to the Black Hills at the request of Chief Henry Standing Bear who said, "My fellow chiefs and I would like the white man to know the red man has great heroes too." The first blast to the mountain occurred on June 3, 1948 and the finished carving of the powerful face of Chief Crazy Horse was dedicated at its completion on June 3, 1998, 50 years later. Although Mr. Ziolkowski died before the monument was completed, the job was turned over to his wife and their children.

On his deathbed, he pleaded with them to "Do the job slowly so that it will get done right."

The clerks in the gift shop were of Indian decent, and when Myndi asked why the Lakota Indian Tribe picked Chief Crazy Horse, they showed her a book that she purchased as a souvenir because in it she found her answer:

Native American leaders chose Crazy Horse for the mountain carving because he was a great and patriotic hero. His tenacity of purpose, his modest life, his unfailing courage, and his tragic death set him apart and above the others. He is a hero not only because of his skill in battle, but also because of his character and his loyalty to his people.

He is remembered for how he cared for the elderly, the ill, the widowed, and the children. His dedication to his personal vision caused him to devote his life to serving his people and to preserving their valued culture. Though he died young, his spirit remains as a role model of selfless dedication and service to others. Today, his values and his story serve as an inspiration for people of all races.

By then it was 5 p.m. With four more hours of good daylight, Myndi decided to drive until she got tired and then locate a motel for the night.

When Myndi got back to the car, she found Ginger asleep in the front passenger seat. She took her for a short walk, gave her water to drink, and put Ginger's fleece blanket on the passenger seat. She was sure she saw a smile come over Ginger's face as she snuggled down for the ride.

From Keystone, they would travel along the northeast border of South Dakota, then through Wyoming, heading in the general direction of Colorado.

Myndi consulted her map and noted that she would have several highway junctions and would need to exit onto various highways. She keyed the directions into her navigator system and, with confidence, headed through Keystone to US 16. Not having a schedule to stick with was a plus. She had already discovered that!

After about thirty minutes on US 16, she noticed a large sign for a Best Western Hotel—the "Cowboy Inn," according to the sign, was located in Custer, South Dakota. The billboard stated, "Just drive two miles." She knew that most Best Western hotels accept pets, and she was already tired from the day's activities, so instead of the long anticipated drive, she decided that—for their safety—it would be best to spend the night at the Cowboy Inn. Besides, the name just sounded like fun.

It was shortly before 6 o'clock when she and Ginger checked into the hotel. The first thing she saw when she opened the drapes of the picture window in their room was the jagged gray of the mountain peaks of the Black Hills of South Dakota. The desk clerk had told her the tallest of the mountains were Harney Peak and Iron Mountain.

She told Myndi that if she was not too tired, the views from nearby Custer State Park, at sunset, were breathtaking. The clerk also said that the gray mountains took on a beautiful purple hue in the evening.

Myndi put dog food in a bowl for Ginger then, for herself, ordered a sandwich, a small bag of potato chips, a cup of coffee, and a double-chocolate chip brownie to go for dessert. She was addicted to chocolate and made sure that her "travel stash" was always replenished. She drove the short distance to Custer Park, found a nice picnic table, and she and Ginger had their dinners and relaxed in the warmth and fresh air of the evening.

Myndi had forgotten to bring her journal to their mini-picnic, so she wrote down notes on the pad she always carried. Later, she would add those pages to her journal.

Myndi's Journal:

Wednesday — June 23

Visiting both Mt. Rushmore and Chief Crazy Horse Monuments was almost too much for me to take in on one day. I could have spent much more time at both of them. I was awed by the majesty of the monuments carved in granite mountains. I will tell the students in my class that I believe these monuments were erected to five great heroes — the Native American Indian, Chief Crazy Horse, and four of our great presidents.

Someone on the photo staff at Mt. Rushmore came out and took a picture of Ginger and me with Mt. Rushmore in the background and then, while I was on tour, they made up a postcard from the photo. I addressed the card and sent it to Grandma Kate.

I also sent her a postcard from the library/gift shop at the Chief Crazy Horse

Monument site. The cards will end up as souvenirs when I get home.

I was glad I made the decision to stay the night in Custer at the Cowboy Inn Hotel. The desk clerk was right about the changing colors of the jagged mountain peaks. The colors ranged from oranges and reds to lavender and then, as the evening began to darken, the hues changed to a beautiful deep purple silhouetted against a blazing yellowish/pink sky. This was a detour I had not planned on taking, but was so glad I did! Of course, I picked up more brochures to add to the already overstuffed box that contains souvenirs for "show and tell" in the classroom.

Myndi had been gone more than a week, and her plan was to see the Rocky Mountains in Colorado before heading home. The next day, Thursday, she would drive the highways she'd already entered into her navigation system en route to Estes Park, Colorado, where she planned to spend two nights. She knew that most of the snow in the lower elevations would be gone by this time of year, so skiing was not an option. She had grown up skiing on Mt. Hood, but in the summertime, hiking the trails was her preferred mode of exercise. She was looking forward to spending time at the famous ski resort.

When Myndi and Ginger returned from their walk in Custer Park, she told the friendly desk clerk that she and her dog were headed for Estes Park, Colorado. The desk clerk, who seemed to be just a couple of years older than Myndi, introduced herself as Helyne and mentioned a bed and breakfast that her grandparents owned in Estes Park.

Helyne said the B&B was a delightful home, with each room decorated with a German/Bavarian influence. She also said there was a great view of the Rocky Mountains from every room. And that her grandparents cooked the breakfasts together and sat with the guests for each morning's feast. "Would you like me to call them and see if they have an opening for Thursday night?" Helyne asked.

Myndi read the brochure about the bed and breakfast and was pleased with the idea. If it worked out, she wouldn't have to look for a room at a hotel or motel when she arrived in Estes Park. By her estimation, the trip tomorrow was going to take at least 8 hours, including rest stops.

Helyne called her grandparents and they confirmed they had a room available and would be happy to have Myndi and Ginger stay with them. They would work out the details when she arrived.

CHAPTER SIX:

ESTES PARK, COLORADO

MYNDI WOKE AT 4 A.M. ON THURSDAY morning, June 24. After her shower and coaxing the sleeping Ginger out for their morning trek, she grabbed a cup of coffee, muffin, and a banana from the breakfast bar, and by 6 o'clock, they were on their way.

Following the navigation directions, they had no problem finding the correct exits and the junctions with other roads. Eventually, they made their way to Interstate 25, the main arterial that would take them to Estes Park.

Myndi was thankful they had spent the night in Custer, because the small towns they cruised through as they drove along this two-hundred-mile stretch of Wyoming did not seem to have any motels. It would definitely have been a mistake if she attempted to complete this part of the journey yesterday evening.

Traveling south down Interstate 25, they arrived in Wheatland, Wyoming, at 10 a.m. That part of the drive had taken them four hours, including the one short stop they made in Shawnee where she found a spot to walk Ginger and gas up at a Plaid Pantry.

In Wheatland, she spotted a mom & pop restaurant and stopped for breakfast. A waitress, coming out as Myndi approached the front door, said that she was on a 20-minute break, and usually took a short walk in the park across the street. "I see you have a dog in your car. Could I take her with me on my walk?"

Myndi and the waitress walked back to Myndi's red Honda Civic. Myndi attached Ginger's leash, then watched as the woman crossed the street into the park. When they were out of sight, she entered the restaurant and ordered breakfast. She was drinking orange juice and reading *USA Today* when the waitress's break ended. Myndi went outside to put Ginger back into her car, then returned to her table just as her breakfast arrived.

The ham and cheese omelet and country-style potatoes were served on a huge platter, way too much for Myndi to eat, so she placed half her meal in a "doggie bag" for Ginger. But she saved room for the homemade biscuit for dessert, which she slathered in a Wild Mountain Blackberry Jam, made by the owners of the mom & pop restaurant.

It was a relief to be out of the car for a while and again Myndi enjoyed eavesdropping on the myriad conversations going on around her as the locals arrived for their breakfasts.

Ginger was at the window wagging her tail enthusiastically when Myndi returned to the car. But she quickly settled down in her passenger seat as they continued south down Interstate 25.

They arrived on the outskirts of Estes Park at 5 p.m. If Myndi had paid more attention to her navigator system, she would not have gotten lost in Cheyenne, Wyoming. That little boo-boo added an additional half-hour to her drive.

Myndi took the Sixth Street exit off Interstate 25,

and after going the ten blocks west, per Helyne's grandparents' instructions, she arrived at the Wagner's bed and breakfast—the Bavarian Alps Chalet. It was as quaint as Helyne had described. Mr. and Mrs. Wagner reminded her of her own grandparents and she immediately felt at home. Her room had a German décor, with a down comforter and crocheted curtains on the wooden slat-covered windows that overlooked the beautiful Rocky Mountain Range. The air was crisp and clear, and the evening walk she and Ginger took was breathtaking.

Thursday—June 24

Ginger and I had such an enjoyable time last night at our "Bonus Overnight" at the Cowboy Inn Motel. Our evening picnic at Custer Park was relaxing and fun as we watched the changing colors of the Rocky Mountains at sunset.

I enjoyed driving the secondary routes this morning rather than taking Interstate 25 in the afternoon. There was so much more to see when I didn't have to focus such close attention on the traffic, even though it was after 6 p.m. by the time we reached our overnight accommodations.

The clerk (Helyne) at the Cowboy Inn told me about her grandparents' bed and breakfast, the Bavarian Alps Chalet, in Estes Park. She called them and made arrangements for Ginger and I to stay here tonight. Mr. & Mrs. Wagner made us feel right at home and said I should look forward to their breakfast "feast" in the morning, but tonight I am still full from today's huge breakfast. Ginger enjoyed my leftovers when we walked this evening.

Tomorrow, I will mail a brochure to you, Grandma, which shows the outside of this bed & breakfast with the Wagners arm-in-arm on the front steps. The photo is so cute, I couldn't resist. They remind me of you and Grandpa.

I am eying the bed with its feather comforter as I write in my journal tonight, looking forward to snuggling down. The Wagner's home is so beautifully furnished. The room décor and decorations, the German music piped throughout the house, and the aromas coming from the kitchen, transport me to another country. I can't help wish that Grandma Kate were here to enjoy this with me. I will put this place down on the list for "must return" trips. I am weary from my drive today, and so glad to be here.

Friday morning's breakfast was everything Myndi had imagined. There were nine people, including the Wagners, at the beautifully set table in a glass-enclosed sunroom. The hand-crocheted tablecloth and matching napkins, and the aroma from a lit candle and the fresh flower centerpiece would make anyone feel welcome in this special place. Breakfast began with fresh-squeezed orange juice and a flaky-crusted apple strudel.

The Wagners insisted that their guests call them by their given names, Karynna and Kurt. You could tell Kurt loved donning his apron as he served a beautiful egg soufflé, hot from the oven, while Karynna brought out ham steaks, sliced tomatoes, baked beans, and warm homemade bread.

Helyne's grandparents told of their life in the Bavarian area of Germany during the war. They had come to America in the late 1940s, explaining how sad it was to leave their elderly parents and their friends. Mr. Wagner's brother and his wife sailed to America at the end of World War II and immediately continued on to Colorado when they arrived in the United States. Their letters back to Germany were so full of praise for their new country that Kurt and Karynna decided to join them. Kurt said it took them two years to complete the paperwork—to get their visas and to prove they had sponsors in America. They also had to prove they had a place of residence once they arrived, which was met by Mr. Wagner's brother and his family. The brother also had a job waiting for them in the German bakery they owned.

In 1960, the Wagners and their young children came to Estes Park on a skiing vacation and they stayed at this very bed and breakfast, which was up for sale at the time. They loved the area and the house, so with the help of Mr. Wagner's brother and his family, they impulsively purchased the property and remodeled the home to reflect the Bavarian atmosphere of Germany.

With their German accents, and the appropriate décor including German furniture, wall hangings, and knick-knacks, one could easily be in Germany. Adding to the ambiance was the beautiful accordion music piped throughout the house and played ever so softly during breakfast.

The conversation went around the table as each of the guests described where they were from. Chantay and David were on vacation from France. Bill and Dotty were attending a business seminar in Denver and had come to Estes Park for a few days of hiking before their return to Florida. Michael and Annette had come to Boulder for their son's college graduation and were making a round of tourist stops nearby before their return to California.

Myndi told them about herself, about her pending marriage to Jeff and new teaching job that would start in September, about her grandmother, Kate, and the graduation gifts Kate had given her. She elaborated on the beauty of Oregon, its coastline, mountains, and the desert region in the eastern part of the state. She talked about her traveling companion, Ginger, asleep in her dog bed upstairs.

Breakfast had begun at 8 o'clock and everyone was shocked at how fast the time had flown when they heard the German grandfather clock in the living room strike ten times. The clock then played a series of German medleys. The departing guests expressed thanks and love to Karynna and Kurt as they left the table and set out on their separate ways.

Myndi had already packed her overnight bags and brought them down to the front entryway before breakfast. She went upstairs and carried Ginger down. Ginger had obviously felt snug and comfy in her surroundings, too. Myndi and Ginger said their goodbyes to Karynna & Kurt, and set off to seek out the lodge the Wagner's said was their favorite of all the Estes Park resorts. Mr. Wagner said his brother still had the bakery in Steamboat Springs, in case Myndi was heading that way.

Long Peak Lodge was located on the banks of Fall River, off Old Fall River Road at the base of the Eastern Slope of the Rocky Mountains. The drive was beautiful as Myndi meandered through Estes Park. She took the time to meander, and stopped to snap a few photos of deer and elk. High up on the mountain she could see big horn sheep. She zoomed in with her digital camera and snapped several photos, which turned out very nice when she viewed them on the camera's display screen.

When they arrived at the lodge at noon, Myndi learned that there were no vacancies except for a small studio room. "Are you interested?" asked the clerk. "The room won't be available until the 3 o'clock, normal check-in time." The lodge was beautiful, so she accepted the room and said she would return about 3 p.m.

She and Ginger went for a short walk around the log lodge and then along the Fall River. The pathway along the riverbank seemed immaculately maintained with native plants, such as ferns, wild bleeding hearts, and lush ground coverings. The aspen trees intermingled with fir trees creating a canopy-like cathedral over the bicycle/hiking trail.

Myndi and Ginger returned to the lodge and entered the large sitting room. She selected a novel from a bookcase, and sat close to the massive rock fireplace, where a crackling fire had been built.

The ceiling was vaulted, and the room was filled with leather and suede furniture of varying colors.

There were comfortable stuffed chairs and rockers, a spacious sofa, and several love seats. Plush area rugs echoed the colors of the furniture and enhanced the light slate-green flooring. Some of the picture windows looked out at the Rocky Mountains; others framed the beauty of the meandering Fall River.

A brochure describing the lodge stated, "In summertime, hiking in the high trails of the mountains replaced wintertime skiing on slopes devoted to the most advanced skiers."

Several other people were taking advantage of the room with its roaring fire. Ginger found a spot next to the rock hearth, and Myndi was comfortable in an overstuffed rocking chair. Two men and two women entered the room. Myndi guessed they were approximately her age and had just come in from a "high country" hike. They removed their coats and hats and made themselves comfortable near the fire. One of the men left, but returned with two bottles of wine, four glasses, and snacks.

They noticed Ginger lying by the fireplace and couldn't help themselves from petting her. Ginger was never one to mind that kind of attention. One of the girls asked Myndi if she would like to join them in a card game and share their wine and snacks. Myndi was still full from her wonderful German breakfast, but said she would relish a glass of wine with them. She loved playing cards, any kind, and wasn't shy about learning new card games.

The foursome introduced Myndi to "Slip & Slide." They said they had stayed up late many nights in college playing the game, after homework was completed, of course. Any number of people could play. However, additional decks of cards had to be added depending on the number playing—five people required two decks. Myndi found Slip & Slide to be a fun game, and as they played, she found out that the four of them were not two couples, but four classmates from the University of Colorado at Boulder. They were from different parts of the country and had become friends during their junior year. They, like herself, had graduated the first week in May, but immediately enrolled in a four-week mini-course on advanced computer programming. Myndi felt homesick as the four friends spoke of their college days. She recalled how excited she and her classmates had been after receiving their diplomas, and the marvelous effect when they all tossed their blue/green caps in the air at the same moment. The caps' silver tassels seemed to glow as they flashed in and out of the overhead spotlights in the auditorium.

One of these young men, Josh, was from the Banff area in Canada. He said he was in the astronaut program at Colorado University. He chose the Boulder location because of the reputation of its space program and said he'd graduated with top grades in most of his courses. It had taken him six years to complete his studies, and had just recently received notification of his acceptance into an apprenticeship program at the Kennedy Space Center in Cape Canaveral, Florida.

Melissa said she had been born and raised in Tampa, Florida, and because she'd had a wonderful teacher in high school geography—a Mrs. Thomas who helped her apply for a partial scholarship to the university—she ended up in Boulder, too. She said she had always wanted to become a teacher, but changed her major midway through and graduated in Criminal Justice. Her goal was to provide assistance to victims, especially in child abuse cases. She had applied at several legal facilities, at the Tampa County courthouse, a few law enforcement agencies, and at two law offices in the Tampa/St. Petersburg area in Florida. She blushed when she said she was happy that Josh was accepting his job assignment in Florida. It would be great to continue their friendship.

Calvin's field was Computer Technology. His hometown was San Diego, California. He had a choice of schools throughout the United States where he could attend, but he chose the University of Colorado at Boulder because of the Rocky Mountains and the winter sports available in the area. He said college had been a challenge for him, but that he excelled in his given field. His desire was to set up a business of his own to assist other businesses in data management, system analysis and design, programming, and website development. One of his great aims was to design a program that would better secure information and transactions when doing business using the Internet.

Andréa said she had always been interested in art, ever since her mother bought her colored pencils and her first box of crayons. She grew up in the Burbank/Hollywood area in California. In grade school, when she was supposed to be paying attention, she would doodle on notebook paper. She doodled whenever talking with friends on the phone using whatever was handy—phonebooks, calendars, anything nearby. It was no surprise to anyone when she chose art, design, and fashion as her elective college courses. Luckily, she received a partial scholarship, but had to supplement that by working. Her expertise now centered on fashion design, film, and photography. She had already received a job offer from Walt Disney Productions, but was waiting for a reply from United Artists studio. She was hoping to get the job at United Artists because of the glamour associated with actors and actresses.

Myndi then related the story of her recent college graduation and the sixth grade geography class she would be teaching in September. She told them about her engagement to Jeff and their wedding plans for next June, about being raised by grandparents, and about the college gift from her grandmother. She expounded on how much fun she was having on the trip, and how neat it was to meet them—such friendly and interesting people.

Josh announced that it was already 3:30, and said what a good time they'd been having talking and playing cards for the past few hours. When they finished their third game of Slip & Slide, Myndi said she had to get her room key, bring in her bags, and take Ginger for another walk along the Falls River pathway. She was thinking of perhaps taking a short nap before dinner.

"There's a happy hour at the bar from five to six every night, how about meeting us there and then us all having dinner together?"

Myndi agreed that was a great idea and said she'd meet them in the bar at 5 o'clock.

After getting her room key at the front desk and walking Ginger, she removed her overnight bag from the back seat of the Honda and went to her studio room. She was surprised when she entered the room because it was so much larger than she had expected. Most of the regular-sized rooms in the hotels and motels she'd stay in along the way were significantly smaller than this one.

The advertisement brochure was sure right when they said the lodge was located at the base of the mountains. The view from her window put her right there. The snow on the mountains, just above the timberline, glistened in the glow of the afternoon sun and she thought of how beautiful the mountains must be when they have their full cover of winter snow.

Myndi had time to freshen up before meeting the others for happy hour. She knew Paula and Scott were due home from their honeymoon today and thought about calling them. But then she decided that perhaps tomorrow would be better. She couldn't wait to tell Paula about her journey so far, what she had seen and done, and all the nice people she'd met all along the way.

Myndi met her four new friends in the lodge bar and they introduced themselves to some of the other guests. The lodge supplied them with finger food to go along with their "happy hour" drinks. They lingered in the bar until 6:30, and then went into the restaurant for dinner. Myndi was hungry; she had indulged in only a few of the finger food items.

The restaurant menu was quite varied which made it difficult to decide what to order, especially with the wonderful smelling aromas coming from the kitchen. The waitress came by to say they had an excellent chicken and dumpling dinner, served family-style, if they were interested. That sounded great to all of them and so it was a unanimous decision.

To accompany their dinner, Myndi ordered a Müeller-Thurgau wine for their table. She told them about her favorite winery in Oregon, located 25 miles west of Portland, and said that the Müller-Thurgau made by that winery was her favorite. She said she was sure they would enjoy it also.

The dinner at the lodge was excellent. It was the "home cooked" meal Myndi had been missing since she had left Jason's, and her new friends agreed that it was most enjoyable. There was dancing after dinner, and Myndi and the other girls took turns dancing with Josh and Calvin, in addition to some of the other overnight guests at the lodge.

When their group found out that Myndi was leaving the next morning, they tried to get her to change her mind and spend one more day with them. But she declined. Myndi had said nothing to them about Jason. They all said their goodnights and goodbyes after exchanging addresses and promises to keep in touch.

Myndi's Journal:

Friday—June 25

It is midnight and I have just finished writing two pages in my journal. It has been a really fun-packed day as you can tell from my writings and one I will remember for a long time. I am writing Grandma a note on the back of a postcard from the Wagner's B&B and sending her one of Long Peak Lodge & Fall River. I also addressed a postcard of the lodge to myself. It will be fun to come across it in the stack of mail waiting for me when I arrive back home.

Myndi reached up to turn out her light when she was interrupted by the ringing of her cell phone. Her sleepy thoughts immediately sprung to her grandmother—*Is Kate okay?*

She was relieved, but confused when a man's voice said, "Hi, Myndi, I'm sorry to call so late, but I just had to see how you are doing."

By then, Myndi was fully awake and began telling Jason about her last several days. She said she would be leaving Estes Park in the morning and heading to Nevada, then up to the Lake Shasta area before heading home. She told him she wanted to be home the following Wednesday.

Jason reminded Myndi about the three-day real estate seminar he was scheduled to attend in Colorado that coming Monday through Wednesday. He said the seminar would be held at the Holiday Inn Resort in Steamboat Springs.

"Myndi," he said, "Can I change your mind about the rest of your trip? Come meet me? We could spend a couple of days together. My plane arrives Sunday afternoon at 4 o'clock and I'll get a shuttle to the hotel. Please, will you meet me there?"

When Myndi heard the name "Steamboat Springs," the same strange chill flashed through her that she'd felt when turning atlas pages at home while planning her trip. With the word "No" forming on her lips, she was surprised when she heard herself saying, "Yes, Jason. A couple of days together sound great. I'll call you when I get there, which will be tomorrow."

Myndi pushed the phone button to disconnect from the call and the realization of what she had just done hit her—why had she agreed to meet Jason? What could she have been thinking? She knew she had just made a terrible decision but at the same time, she was excited about seeing him again!

CHAPTER SEVEN:

STEAMBOAT SPRINGS, COLORADO

IT WAS SATURDAY, JUNE 26 and Myndi and Ginger woke up at 5 o'clock. After her shower and one more walk along the Fall River path, she grabbed a bite to eat at the continental breakfast bar and loaded her luggage and Ginger into the car.

She consulted her road map and thought it looked like a straight shot from Estes Park to Steamboat Springs, but she wondered about the effect of the Rocky Mountains on the curvy roads that her route would take. She added up the mileage and estimated the driving time from Estes Park to Steamboat Springs would be four hours.

Why am I feeling such a strong a pull from Steamboat Springs? Myndi wondered. It wasn't just

Jason's phone call last night. She had never been to Steamboat Springs before, and she didn't even know anyone who had been there except for the brother Mr. Wagner had spoken about and the bakery he owned.

Myndi headed out of Estes Park on US 34. The road traversed Rocky Mountain National Park and it turned out to be an incredibly winding but beautiful route that skirted the mountains. She continued on US 34 and found out that the last 60 miles was on the edge of the Arapaho National Forest.

She stopped several times so that she and Ginger could stretch their legs and to take a moment to just observe the beauty that surrounded them. Finally, at Granby, they came to the junction with US 40 and it turned out to be a much straighter road. She relaxed her tensed neck and back muscles, and loosened her grip on the steering wheel. She estimated that from this junction they probably had another 80 miles before arriving in Steamboat Springs.

They had left Estes Park at around 8 o'clock that

morning and reached the outskirts of Steamboat Springs at 1:30. The drive had been exhausting. She didn't know what the next couple of days had in store for her with Jason's arrival, but she decided to skip Nevada and Lake Shasta and head for home once she left this town.

Myndi continued on US 40 and easily found the Holiday Inn Resort. She parked at the front entrance and went into the lobby. Check-in time was not until 3 o'clock, so she reserved a room for two nights. She needed to regroup and make plans for her route home. She hadn't done any laundry since leaving Paula's, but figured she could get it done first thing in the morning, before Jason's arrival that afternoon.

While she waited for her room to become available, she drove to the Chamber of Commerce. Summertime activities were in effect here, just as they had been in Estes Park. The Chamber provided her with a list of events and activities scheduled for June, which included a gondola ride to the top of the mountain, bicycling along the paths, and outdoor concerts. It also provided a list of sites designated for mineral baths. When registering at the Holiday Inn, she had also noticed their inviting outdoor swimming pool.

Myndi had seen the gondolas going up the mountain when she drove into town and thought it might be a fun way to spend time before getting her room key. Each of the gondolas held eight people. She was allowed to take Ginger with her as long as she held her while they were in the gondola, and put her on a leash once they got to the top.

The Mt. Werner Gondola ride afforded Myndi a bird's eye view of this part of Colorado as it crossed over meadows strewn with wildflowers and groves of aspen trees. She looked down on the town of Steamboat Springs and had a panoramic view of the surrounding hillsides. Once on top, she found the cool mountain breeze utterly refreshing. She was glad she took the advice of the clerk at the Chamber and brought along a sweater. An indoor/outdoor café was situated on top of the mountain, so she ordered a grilled chicken sandwich, French fries, and a cup of their house specialty—chicken fiesta soup. The soup was piping hot and topped with cheese, onions, and broken tortilla chips.

Myndi had brought along a couple of dog biscuits for Ginger, but instead she shared some of her chicken and French fries with her and then, after she had finished her soup, poured some water for Ginger into the paper soup bowl.

Several people getting off the gondola headed for the bicycle shop next to the café. They rented bikes and headed out along the many different surrounding paths. Myndi was content to just people-watch, happy to be free from sitting behind the steering wheel of her car.

The ride up the mountain had taken 20-minutes, so after spending an hour on top, she and Ginger returned to the gondola for the trip down. She had to chuckle to herself when she recalled how Jeff hated height. He loved to ski, but he wouldn't even take the ski lift at Mt. Hood, nor could she get him on a Ferris wheel when they attended the Oregon State Fair.

It was 5 o'clock by the time they got to her room

and brought in her overnight luggage. She figured it was a good time to check out the heated outdoor swimming pool. So, she retrieved Ginger's blanket from the car and the two of them headed for the pool. It was still early enough in the evening that most people were busy doing other activities, so Myndi had the pool pretty much to herself. It was a warm June evening and she was taken in by the beauty of the surrounding Rocky Mountains, even though only a skiff of snow remained near the tops of the peaks.

Alone with her thoughts, she couldn't help wonder why she had been feeling so uneasy about Steamboat Springs. She certainly had not felt any uneasiness since arriving in town.

Back in the room by 7 o'clock, Myndi decided to call Paula and ask how their honeymoon played out. When Paula answered, she said that she and Scott had returned Friday evening and that they'd had a wonderful time in Victoria, British Columbia in Canada. On the ferry ride from Port Angeles to Victoria, they saw Orca whales. They'd met an older couple who told them about a quaint bed and breakfast cottage in downtown Victoria—the couple had just spent three nights with the owner and her husband and they'd had a truly enjoyable time. They gave Paula a brochure from the cottage. Paula said she and Scott checked it out and spent two of their five nights there. The owner was from Austria and most of the antique furniture, lace curtains, doilies, and china had belonged to her mother. The owner said she had it all shipped from Austria to Victoria after purchasing the bed and breakfast.

Paula spoke of their afternoon "high" tea at the Empress Hotel, and the railroad museum in the heart of downtown Victoria. She said they spent two days at the Butchart Gardens, and then traveled north on the island to do some deep-sea fishing.

Myndi told Paula she was calling from Steamboat Springs, Colorado, and recounted her trip and all the places she'd visited since leaving Kellogg.

Then Paula said, "Myndi, Scott and I had lunch with Jason this afternoon and he told us he has fallen in love with you. He also said he was meeting you in Steamboat Springs, something about a three-day seminar he had to attend there. What happened between you and Jason after we left for our honeymoon?"

Myndi couldn't keep it locked inside any longer. She told Paula exactly what had happened between her and Jason, but asked her to please not say anything to anyone until she returned home and could sit down and confess her indiscretion to Jeff. She had no explanation for her actions, but she did admit she was very enamored with Jason and had been experiencing anxiety about what she'd done.

Paula said she understood, but wondered where Myndi stood in relation to Jason because he had seemed so dejected when they'd seen him at lunch.

"I've tried to put Jason out of my mind. But he called me last night and asked me to meet him in Steamboat Springs. I agreed to do it. But I'm so confused about this and will have to deal with the situation when I get home. All I know is that I have to see Jason again."

"I know how much you and Jeff love each other,

Myndi. So call me anytime you feel the need to talk about this."

Myndi felt so thankful for Paula. She had needed someone to talk to this past week, but couldn't tell anyone. It felt good to get the secret off her chest. Paula was the friend she needed.

After they hung up, Myndi wrote a short page in her journal then crawled into bed with a novel. She barely got through three pages before she laid the book on the nightstand. That's when she noticed a guestbook next to the telephone. She had made it a practice to sign guestbooks whenever proprietors of the motels and inns left one for their guests.

Myndi found it fun to read what other people had written and liked to think that others would enjoy her words, too. She dropped off to sleep promising that she would write in this guestbook before leaving Steamboat Springs.

Myndi's Journal:

> *Saturday—June 26*
>
> *The scenery on our trip to Steamboat Springs from Estes Park was a beautiful, but hard drive since the secondary roads were so curvy. Highway 40 into Steamboat Springs afforded more relaxation and I was able to take in more of the scenery of the national forests and the Rocky Mountain views. Ginger and I had a fun time on our gondola ride up Mt. Werner, and my evening swim in the hotel's pool was wonderful. Our room at the Holiday Inn overlooks the Rockies and I never tire of seeing them because their colors change from early morning to dawn, and at night you feel even closer to the mountains with the hotel spotlights shining on the slopes. I called Paula this evening. We had a good chat about their honeymoon and I told her of the things I had seen and done since leaving Kellogg.*

My postcard to Grandma today was of the gondola. I know she will show it to Jeff and he will probably just shake his head at the thought!

Myndi and Ginger took their early morning walk before Myndi went to eat in the hotel's continental breakfast room. It was already Sunday, June 27. She fixed herself a bowl of cereal, toast, and a cup of coffee.

She met a young couple who invited her to join them at their table. They were from Albany, New York. Their plans this morning were to take a bicycle ride alongside the nearby stream. Myndi thought that sounded like fun and asked if she could accompany them. They finished eating, then at 8:30 they met in the lobby and checked out bicycles. Myndi found one with a front basket so she could take Ginger along. The couple rented a bicycle built for two. Several people were already bicycling on the path, and after a 45-minute ride, the three of them took a brief break to rest on the banks of the stream.

The morning air was cool and refreshing. They continued on their ride for a while longer, then Myndi and Ginger returned to the hotel. Myndi wanted to catch up on her laundry.

On the bike ride back to the hotel, Myndi made the decision to spend one more night in Steamboat Springs with Jason. When she turned in her bicycle, she learned that a mountain concert would be taking place that evening, and that the hotel restaurant was hosting a barbeque dinner and sing-along. She signed up for two people, anticipating Jason would want to attend, and signed herself up for a two-hour outdoor china-painting class that afternoon from 1 to 3 o'clock. A couple of decorated plates were on display and she thought a hand-painted plate made by her would be a fun souvenir to take back to Grandma Kate.

Myndi gathered her dirty clothes from the room, and the bundle she'd kept in a separate bag in the trunk of the car, then headed for the guest laundry room. She'd taken her novel with her, so read while her clothes washed and dried. After folding most of the items, and hand pressing her tee shirts and shorts, she returned to her room. She was tired of living out of a suitcase, and planned to stay another night, so she began placing her newly washed clothes in the dresser drawers. She put her underwear in the top left-hand drawer and her tee shirts and shorts in the top right-hand drawer.

When she opened the tee-shirt drawer, to her surprise she found a beautifully framed gold leaf etched photograph. She lifted the frame to look closer, but almost fainted when she saw that the woman in the photo was of herself and two children. She sat on the edge of the bed staring at the picture in disbelief, for how long she did not know. She turned the frame over hoping to see a name, but there was none. She removed the photo from the frame and turned that over, expecting to find some kind of indication as to who the woman was. There was nothing. No clue. How could anyone have known she would be here? Who could have played this kind of trick on her! No matter how hard she tried, she couldn't believe what she held in her hand.

Grasping the frame tightly, she darted down the three flights of stairs to the front desk. Several couples were checking in so she had to wait. She shifted impatiently from one foot to the other. She caught herself biting her lower lip, a nervous habit. The palms of her hands began sweating, and she was shaking so hard she could hardly remain standing. Yet there it was again, those icy chills running down her spine, adding to her confusion and discomfort.

The clerk finally finished her transactions with the arriving guests and asked how she could help. Myndi blurted out, "Can you tell me who the people were that rented Room #323 before me?"

The young clerk said she had just come on shift that morning after three days off, but she could look up that information.

"Of course the room has been rented to several people over the past several months. Is something wrong with the room?"

Myndi showed the photograph to the clerk who commented on how beautiful she and her two children were. Myndi was shocked when she realized someone else thought she was the woman in the photo.

"I am NOT the woman in the photo," Myndi said.

"I have no idea who this woman is, nor anything about these two children."

By this time, the hotel manager, who had overheard the conversation, walked over to the counter to assist. Myndi explained how she'd found the photo in the dresser drawer in her room upstairs and that she had to find out the names and addresses and phone numbers of the guests who had occupied Room #323. The manager was very sympathetic, but stated that hotel policy did not allow him to give out personal addresses of hotel guests, those presently residing and those who had been guests in the past.

By this time, Myndi was frantic. "Then what can I do?" she pleaded.

The manager said they had recently remodeled that room, replacing the carpeting and the old furniture. He sympathized with her anguish, but could offer no suggestions other than leaving the framed photograph with them and if possible, they would try to track down the owner.

"No way," replied Myndi. "I have the picture in

my possession and I will not give it up. I need to solve this mystery. And you need to give me the names and contact information for all the guests who recently stayed in Room 323."

After a twenty-minute conversation with the home office, the manager returned to the counter and said he would give her the names of the guests, but due to hotel policy and privacy acts, he could provide no other assistance.

Myndi left the lobby with the names of three couples, two men, and *the photograph!*

She returned to her room and immediately placed a call to Jeff. There was a long silence on his end of the phone after she explained what had transpired over the past few hours. Jeff could offer no advice, but he agreed that she needed to end the trip and come home immediately. He asked if she wanted him to take the next flight out of Portland and meet her in Steamboat Springs so he could be with her for her drive back home. Myndi considered telling him yes, but instead said that the hotel had given her some information about the previous five occupants of the room and that she had already packed her suitcases and would be leaving Steamboat Springs as soon as she could check out. She told Jeff she loved him for wanting to be with her for the trip back to Oregon, and that she would take the shortest route possible.

"Jeff, can you think of any way I can research these names? Could you relate this story to the partners in your law firm and ask for their assistance? Would you call Grandma Kate and tell her about the photo and that I'm heading home? And tell her I love her."

Myndi had one thought in mind, and that was to get back home as quickly as possible. She spread out her maps on the bed and figured she could get in at least five hours travel time before having to spend the night somewhere. It appeared her route would take her from US 40, to the junction with US 189, and then onto US 90 through Salt Lake City.

She had no idea where to start, or how to go about finding the lady in the photograph, but as she gathered the maps and reached for her novel on the nightstand, she spotted the guestbook. She opened it to the first blank page and pondered a moment, thinking how she could relate her story about the framed photograph. She decided to avoid that topic and simply wrote down how pretty the area was and the fun she and Ginger had on the gondola. She signed her name, wrote down her address, and began to close the book when the thought struck her, *I just signed my name and address!*

She began flipping back through the pages. The entry before hers was a man from Michigan, Dale Henry. He had spent only one night. On the page before him, was a note from Kevin & Carolyn Lee from Missoula, Montana. They had spent three nights. Another couple left a note after spending one night, Brad and Karen Matthews. They were vacationing from Las Vegas. Paul Kaufmann, from Randegg, Germany, wrote that he'd attended a four-day seminar on telecommunications. And, another couple, Elizabeth and Mark Rogers, wrote that their time in Steamboat Springs was wonderfully relaxing on both the days they spent here. They had not included an address, but they did say the mountains here were equal in beauty to their Canadian Rockies, near their hometown of Banff.

Myndi couldn't believe her luck. She had addresses for three of the five prior guests in this room. She jotted down all the information each of them wrote on the guestbook pages. This stroke of luck would be an immense aid in her search. As she puzzled over all the facts coming together, she couldn't help but wonder, *Why was I really meant to be on this trip? Why in this place? Why at this time?*

By then, it was a few minutes past noon. She was visibly shaking when she went down to the front desk and checked out. That's when she remembered Jason was about to arrive. She asked for a sheet of the hotel stationary and wrote:

Dear Jason,

I am sorry I had to leave before you arrived. I really had planned to be with you here, but a problem has arisen and I need to get back home as soon as possible. I will call you with the full explanation soon. Forgive me.

Fondly,
Myndi

She put the note in an envelope, addressed to Jason, and asked the desk clerk to give it to him when he checked in later that afternoon.

Consulting her navigation system once more after keying in her destination proved her selected route to be the best option. She made sure Ginger was comfortable in her passenger seat, buckled herself in, and left. She stopped at a gas station in Steamboat Springs to fill up the tank before heading out of town. As soon as she was on the open road, she focused all her attention on getting to Heber City, Utah.

Her navigation system predicted a 300-mile trip, taking approximately five hours. She added an hour for rest stops for herself and Ginger.

The trip along US 40 was uneventful. There were a couple of places where highway work was in progress and, except for when her mind strayed to the mystery of the photograph, she concentrated on the road ahead.

She was still in Colorado, about two hours out from Steamboat Springs, when she came to the little town of Elk Springs. She stopped for a potty break for Ginger and found a drive-in hamburger restaurant where she purchased a burger, fries, and a small strawberry shake, which she ate as she continued angling her way northwest along US 40.

It was 6:30 p.m. when she arrived in Heber City, Utah. It had taken her longer than expected and she was very tired, in both her mind and body, but proud that she had made her planned destination. Her navigation system responded to her inquiry about motels in Heber City by directing her down South Main Street. She had no trouble locating Mac's Motel. She checked into a room and then took Ginger for a short walk to a nearby park.

On the way back to the motel, she passed a restaurant where the aroma of pizza was insistent. Although she was really too exhausted to eat, she stopped and ordered one piece of pizza to go, along with a soft drink, figuring it would taste good later.

Once back in her room, she took a warm shower then dried her hair. She called Grandma Kate to tell her she was okay, just tired. They had a short conversation. Myndi said she was going to get some sleep, and that she planned to rise early the next morning to get in as much driving time on Monday as possible. Grandma Kate was full of questions based on the scanty information Jeff had told her, but Myndi said she would fill in the details when she arrived back home.

Myndi's Journal:

Sunday—June 27

So very much has occurred today and I am way too tired to make entries in my journal tonight. However, the biggest surprise was the mystery surrounding the photograph in the chest of drawers in my room at the Holiday Inn, in Steamboat Springs. It is a color photo of a woman who looks to be my age. The woman has the same auburn hair and green eyes as I have. The truth is, I am quite shaken by today's episode, and I've made up my mind to get back home as quickly as possible to find answers to the puzzling questions spinning in my brain. Steamboat Springs is a pretty area. The gondola ride was a fun experience and perhaps someday a vacation here would be enjoyable. This whole trip has been really pleasurable, but it would have been better to have shared the experience with a companion.

Chapter Eight:

Utah To Idaho

AFTER RISING EARLY ON MONDAY, JUNE 28, and taking Ginger for her morning walk, Myndi consulted her maps and guessed that she was a little over twelve hours from Portland. Her estimate included rest stops. She decided to split the travel time into two six-hour days. In her estimation, today's route would place her in Boise, Idaho, where she would spend the night.

Her room at Mac's Motel was comfortable, and located right in the downtown area of Heber City. They did not offer a continental breakfast, but there was a coffeemaker in her room. She made a pot of strong coffee and filled her thermos for the trip. By the time she showered, checked out, and loaded her luggage back in the car, it was 7 a.m. She consulted her navigator system, keyed in the information, and discovered that she would be traveling north on US

40 to exit 148, then on Interstate 84 to exit 168, and then on Interstate 80 in order to arrive in Ogden, Utah. She wouldn't have to go through the larger city of Salt Lake. However, had she not been in such a hurry to get home, it would have been nice to see the Mormon Tabernacle and hear the choir perform. She knew it was famous worldwide for the singers' resounding voices.

Myndi had gone about forty miles when she began to get hungry. So before her exit off Interstate 80, she stopped in Echo, a tiny town. Searching for a restaurant for breakfast, she found herself on Aspen Drive. She couldn't believe it when she drove up to the No Worries Café & Grill. She ordered a bowl of oatmeal, which was piping hot when it arrived at her table. She ordered her favorite toppings— raisins, brown sugar, cinnamon, and Half & Half. She saved her piece of toast, which she smothered in fresh strawberry jam, to eat when she drank her coffee. She read the outside cover of the menu, which told the history of the town. Echo began in 1854 as a stagecoach stop. In 1860, the pony express also built a station here, and in 1868, when the railroad lines were laid through the middle of town, Echo grew rapidly. However, the 1929 stock market crash and the ensuing depression years forced many people to move away because there was no real industry in the town.

Along Interstate 84, she and Ginger stopped at a rest stop to stretch their legs before continuing on to Ogden, which was only a half-hour from Echo. From Ogden, she planned to drive Interstate 84 to Boise, which, according to the navigation system, was 304.3 miles from Ogden, and would take four hours and twelve minutes to get there. Myndi thought, *How cool is that!*

By then it was 11 o'clock. Traffic was light as they traveled northwest on Interstate 84. Myndi listened to her favorite CDs, and sang along as she tried to keep her mind off the mysterious photo and how to tell Jeff about Jason. Jason was the furthest thing from her mind.

Six hours into the trip from Ogden, which of course included a couple of rest stops, they reached the outskirts of Boise, Idaho. It was a much bigger town than Myndi had expected and the 5 o'clock rush hour was in full force, so she decided to drive on just a bit further. She was a half-hour beyond Boise city limits when she noticed a road sign for a La Quinta Inn in Caldwell, Idaho. Myndi didn't want to push herself any further, so she checked herself and Ginger in for the night. It was a nice clean room and the Inn was within walking distance to the Boise River. After taking her overnight bag up to her room and getting Ginger's bed fluffed for the night, Myndi took out her journal and recorded the day's travels. Then she and Ginger took a leisurely stroll on the path alongside the Boise River.

On the way back to the Inn, she stopped at a drive-in and picked up a chicken sandwich, fries, and a milk shake to go. She turned on the television in her room and watched the evening news as she ate her dinner. She was in bed by 8:30 and fast asleep by 9 o'clock.

Myndi's Journal:

> *Monday—June 28*
>
> *The road trip today was on freeways. I guess I didn't pay too much attention to the surrounding countryside because my mind was on so many other things, including paying attention to the other cars on the Interstate. I certainly enjoyed my little detour in Echo, Utah, when I stumbled across a wonderful restaurant for breakfast. The thought crossed my mind that it was there just for me. I chuckled most of the day about the name, No Worries Café & Grill. Tomorrow I will travel the last leg of my journey before getting back home. I will even gain an hour as I go from Mountain Time to Pacific Time.*

CHAPTER NINE:

IDAHO TO HOME

IT WAS 6 A.M. ON TUESDAY, JUNE 29 when Myndi woke to discover that she had left the television on all night. *Boy, I must have really zonked out!* She had wanted to be on the road earlier, so she hurriedly took her shower and ate a continental breakfast. Then she took Ginger for a short romp, loaded the car, and checked out of the motel.

She thought about going from Ontario, a town just across the Idaho border in Oregon, to Salem, but decided to check with her navigation system to determine the shortest route. The route from Ontario to Salem was 420 miles, estimated to take five hours and fifty-two minutes travel time. It would take one more hour to go from Salem to Portland. But the route from Ontario to Portland along Interstate 84 was far shorter. The navigation system estimated it was 374.8 miles—fifty miles shorter. Driving time along the Columbia River on Interstate 84 was predicted to take five hours and nine minutes, also shorter, but not by much. After weighing the two options, she decided to take Interstate 84 the rest of the way home.

Travel time from Caldwell, Idaho, to Ontario, Oregon, was estimated to take twenty-seven minutes. It would be a long trip today, but perhaps it wouldn't seem as long since she would gain an hour due to the time zone change.

She text-messaged Jeff from her cell phone that she was in Caldwell, Idaho, and that, according to her navigation system, including the one-hour time change and a few rest stops along the way, she could arrive home as early as 2:30 p.m.

It was 7:30 a.m. by the time she pulled out of the parking lot of the La Quinta Inn and onto Interstate 84. She told Ginger, "We're going home today!" She wondered if Ginger was as happy as she was.

A short half hour later, they crossed the border

into Oregon. The rest of the trip would be accomplished on sheer adrenalin. To get from Ontario to Boardman, they sped through Baker City, La Grande, and then Pendleton.

They had stopped twice at rest stops to stretch and take their potty breaks. One of the rest stops offered free coffee and cookies. Myndi poured coffee into her thermos, left a dollar in the tip jar, and they were off again.

The trip from Caldwell, Idaho, to Boardman, Oregon had taken four hours, but with the time change, it was still only 10:30 a.m.

In Boardman, Myndi was back on familiar ground. The trip along the Columbia River to Portland was one of her favorite drives. The river was often referred to as the "Mighty Columbia," and to Myndi it was all that and more. The river was absolutely beautiful as it cut its way through deep canyons and formed the border between Oregon and Washington.

By noon, Myndi drove into The Dalles to gas up and get a bite to eat. She stopped at a diner and ordered a turkey sandwich and cup of soup. She'd had enough coffee for one day. Thirty minutes later, she was back on Interstate 84. She'd be home in less than two hours.

At 2 o'clock, Myndi pulled into her driveway. She was surprised that she had come so close to her estimated time of arrival. She'd been on her trip two weeks to the day. It seemed like she had been gone a month, and in some respects, the trip seemed like it had taken a lifetime.

Grandma Kate came to the front door when she heard the Honda in the driveway. Ginger bounded out of the car and, with tail wagging, scurried up the stairs to greet her. Myndi was right behind her as she rushed to hug and kiss her grandmother.

Myndi knew Grandma Kate would be full of questions, but Myndi was so exhausted that all she wanted to do right then was stretch out for an hour nap. Grandma said a nap was a good idea because that way she could talk to Jeff, too. She had already invited Jeff to dinner that evening and he was planning to arrive straight from work.

Myndi didn't even take the time to unpack the car. She showered, then crawled beneath the covers of her own bed. It felt so good to be home.

It was 5 o'clock when she awoke from her nap. She knew Jeff would probably arrive about 5:30. Grandma Kate had dinner prepared and the table set when Myndi came downstairs.

Myndi was waiting for Jeff at the door when he pulled up at 5:40 pm. She threw her arms around him and began crying. Jeff was happy she was so glad to see him. He had missed her, too.

While they ate dinner, Myndi showed them the framed photograph of the woman and two children and they, too, were shocked at the twin image of Myndi that smiled back at them from the photo. If anyone had some kind of answer to the puzzle, Myndi figured that that person would be her grandmother, but Grandma Kate was speechless. It was as much a mystery to her as it was to Myndi.

Myndi brought out her copies of the guestbook pages and the three of them began to brainstorm how to go about finding the identity of person in the photo. Jeff had mentioned some of the details to his senior partners and they offered the use of company computers and legal advice if needed. Myndi, of course, had been thinking about a plan for the past couple of days as she drove home. She would start her research in the morning, beginning by entering the names and addresses she had on the Internet in the hope of finding leads.

Myndi and Jeff spent the rest of the evening unpacking the Honda. Jeff brought in two boxes of brochures, history books, and souvenirs as Myndi eagerly told of all the exciting things she'd encountered along her trip. Well, almost everything. She would wait until the moment was right before she said anything about Jason, but for some reason she was not feeling guilty about what had gone on between them. It had been a sweet experience and even now, after seeing and holding Jeff, she was not ashamed of what she had done. She only hoped Jeff would understand. Meanwhile, she still needed time to sort out the deep feelings she had for Jason.

Myndi's journal writings for the last several

days of her travels had been relatively short, revealing only her time spent at rest stops, hotels, and the number of hours she spent in road travel each day. Gone was the excitement of seeing new places, taking advantage of tourist areas, and meeting new people.

CHAPTER TEN:

THE SEARCH BEGINS

MYNDI WAS UP EARLY THE MORNING of Wednesday, June 30. She had spent an hour last night researching the hotel guests' names on the Internet, and arranging the data she had gathered for the people she would contact.

After breakfast, Myndi rehearsed and wrote down some of the things she wanted to say to the people on her list. She began her search with the easiest of the names, a call to Dale Henry in Michigan.

A woman answered.

"Is this the Dale Henry residence?" Myndi asked.

"Yes," the woman said.

Myndi quickly explained who she was and that she had spent some time recently in Steamboat

Springs, Colorado. She had decided that there was no need to go into mysterious details of how much the woman in the photo resembled her.

"From the guestbook in the Holiday Inn room I occupied, I wrote down the information penned by Dale Henry because I found an eight by ten inch framed photo in one of the dresser drawers and I wonder if perhaps it was left by Mr. Henry."

"I don't think so," the woman replied.

"The photo is of a woman and two young children, a boy and a girl."

"I am Mrs. Henry. My husband and I spent one night at Steamboat Springs on our way to Utah to spend some time with my mother-in-law after her brief hospital stay. The photo is not ours. We brought in just one small valise for the overnight stay and did not bring any photos along on the trip. But thank you for calling. I hope you find the owner of the photo."

"Thank you for your time, Mrs. Henry, I do have four other names to contact."

Myndi crossed off the first name from her list.

Myndi's second call was to Kevin and Carolyn Lee and the response was similar. After relating her story of finding the photo, and how she saw their names in the hotel's guestbook, Carolyn Lee said, "Yes we did unpack and use the dresser for our belongings. We spent the last three days of our honeymoon in Steamboat Springs. However, we didn't have any framed photos with us on our trip."

"Thank you for your help, Mrs. Lee," Myndi said. "I hope you have a wonderful summer and congratulations on your marriage."

When Myndi called the residence of the Matthews, the third number on her list, she received their answering machine which stated, "Thank you for calling Brad and Karen. We are away from the phone right now. Please leave your name and phone number, plus a brief message and we will return your call as soon as one of us returns."

Myndi's message provided her name and phone number and a brief statement about finding a framed photograph in the dresser drawer at the Holiday Inn Resort in Steamboat Springs. "Please call me when you get a moment." Myndi hung up the phone and then sat back feeling more anxious and apprehensive than when she started her search earlier that morning.

Myndi sat staring at the next name on her list—Paul Kaufmann, in Germany. He had left no phone number or address, only that he was from Randegg, Germany. Myndi knew this search was going to take some time.

By then it was lunchtime and she need a break from the nervous stress she was feeling, so she went downstairs to get a bite to eat and relax. She found Grandma Kate in the backyard. She had just finished picking a bouquet of roses, enough to fill two vases—one for the coffee table in the living room, and the other for the dining room table centerpiece. The roses were lovely and would soon fill the whole house with their beautiful aroma.

Jeff called during their lunch for a progress report. "I'm sure glad you are so upbeat, Myndi," he said. "I was afraid if you didn't find something right away you would be discouraged. I love you, honey.

I'm so glad you're home. I missed you while you were gone."

"I love you too, Jeff. Will you come by after work? How about dinner with Grandma Kate and me?"

"Great, Myndi, see you around 6 o'clock."

Myndi and Grandma Kate were finishing their lunch when Myndi brought up the name of Paul Kaufmann in Germany. She said she was perplexed about how to go about finding a phone number or address for him. Grandma Kate thought about it for a minute and then came up with an idea. "Myndi," she said, "Remember your pen pal, Krista? Didn't she live in Germany? Perhaps she could help you."

Myndi ran around the table and hugged her grandmother. "What a great idea," she said, and kissed Grandma Kate on the forehead. She cleared the table and while tidying the kitchen, she laid plans for contacting Krista.

When Myndi was in the fourth grade, her teacher, Mrs. Anderson, the same person who had suggested the class keep a daily journal, had also arranged a pen pal project. She had a list of names of boys and girls in Europe, and some in the United States, who had indicated a desire to receive and write letters back and forth to people their own age. Some of the kids in Myndi's class didn't want to participate and Mrs. Anderson had said the activity was totally optional. It would not affect their grades if they chose not to participate, she said. But she did encourage them. She said writing to someone in another part of the world would often gain them a lifelong friend and that they would definitely learn about new places.

Myndi had looked over the names on Mrs. Anderson's list and settled on Krista, who was the same age and in the same grade. She and her family lived in Munich, Germany, which was another reason for Myndi's choice. Myndi knew her ancestors had come from Germany. The two girls hit it off right from the start.

In Myndi's first letter to Krista, she mentioned her grade school and friends. She told her about her parents and brother, who had been killed in an auto accident, and how she came to be raised by her grandparents. All through their years, the two girls corresponded with monthly letters, gifts on their birthdays, and Christmas packages. They exchanged school pictures throughout grade school, high school, and college. Krista knew all about Jeff, and she shared news about a boy she had been dating.

During their last year at college, Krista had attended a Finishing School in Munich, and their letter correspondence ebbed, although they did keep in contact through occasional emails.

After finishing the dishes from lunch, Myndi bounded up the stairs. She would try calling Krista. An email would leave too much unsaid.

By then it was 2:30 and Myndi remembered the eleven-hour difference between Oregon and Munich time. By her calculation, it was 1:30 in the morning in Germany—much too early to disturb her friend, even with her sense of urgency.

She opened the Internet Explorer search engine on her computer and typed in "Randegg, Germany."

She learned it was a small town in the southern area of Germany, approximately 45-miles from Zurich, Switzerland. A search in the Internet phone directory turned up no match for "Paul Kaufman," so she just printed out the brief information about the town.

Time had rapidly slipped away as Myndi continued her research, but a phone call at 4:30 roused her. Myndi's heart skipped a beat when the caller introduced herself as Karen Matthews. Myndi blurted out her story about finding the photograph and then coming across their address in the guestbook in Room #323 at the Holiday Inn Resort.

When she finished, Karen Matthews said she knew nothing about the photo, but wished Myndi success in her search. She did mention, however, that when her husband, Brad, was checking them out of the hotel, she had met a woman who said that they had just flown in from Banff, Canada. Karen said the woman and her husband appeared to be about 50 years old. "They were on their way back home after attending a nephew's college graduation from the University of Colorado at Boulder."

Josh's face quickly came into view, but Myndi erased the thought. Josh was one of the four friends she'd met at the Long Peak Lodge in Estes Park. Could the couple Karen met have been Josh's parents traveling from Banff? Had Josh mentioned his parents flew in for his graduation? *Too bizarre!* Myndi thought. *Too coincidental!*

She thanked Mrs. Matthews for the return call and the information. Her head was reeling and her hands were shaking as she returned the phone to its base.

Myndi picked up her journal and searched for the page where she had jotted down the names and addresses of the four friends she'd ended up playing cards and dancing with. Josh's last name was Miller. She had his address and phone number in Banff. She knew it would be an unlikely coincidence, but something was nudging her on, compelling her to check out yet another phase of the mystery.

Nervously, she dialed the number Josh had given her. It connected to his parent's home, the only way to contact him before he arrived in Florida. Myndi introduced herself when a woman answered the phone. She said she had met her son, Josh, in Estes Park shortly after his graduation and that she'd had fun spending time with him and his three fellow classmates.

The woman introduced herself as Julia Miller and said she'd spoken to Josh after his trip to Estes Park. She said Josh, too, had mentioned the fun time he'd had while there.

Then Myndi explained that she'd found a photograph while staying at the Holiday Inn in Steamboat Springs, was trying to locate the person who'd left it there, and asked if Julia might check her Banff phone book for a listing for Elizabeth and Mark Rogers.

"Mark Rogers is my brother and Elizabeth is my sister-in-law. They live just a couple of blocks from us and yes, they went on to Steamboat Springs after Josh's graduation." She gave Myndi their phone number and said how happy she was that Myndi had called. She also said she had just spoken to Josh the evening before. He had found a small studio apartment and was attending his first orientation meeting today. She said she would tell him about her conversation with Myndi the next time they spoke.

Myndi placed the call to the Rogers. Mark Rogers answered the phone and Myndi spent a few minutes repeating the reason for her call.

Mark Rogers' response was disappointing. "Yes, Elizabeth and I stayed at the Holiday Inn Resort in Steamboat Springs. And yes, it is possible our room was number 323. But I know nothing about a photograph, and we didn't place anything in the bureau drawers."

Well, Myndi thought as she hung up the phone. *That certainly was an odd coincidence.*

Jeff arrived just as Myndi headed downstairs. He sat at the kitchen table sipping a beer while the two women prepared dinner. He listened intently as Myndi recounted the results of her phone calls.

Myndi felt her options were running out. It seemed her last chance to find an answer to the mystery of the photograph lay with Paul Kaufman.

Jeff left about 8:30 p.m. Myndi finished cleaning up the dinner dishes and made her way upstairs to call her pen pal, Krista.

It was 8 a.m. in Munich when Krista answered the phone. She said she was just heading out the door on her way to work. But Myndi chatted on and on, hitting the high spots of all that had happened. She told Krista about the only remaining name on her list and the few facts she knew about "Paul Kaufman."

Krista said she knew almost nothing about Randegg, only that it was a small town located near Switzerland and very close to Lake Constance, in the southern Germany area. Myndi told Krista that Paul Kaufman had written of a telecommunication seminar he had attended in Steamboat Springs and asked if she might have any ideas of where or how to continue her search.

Krista said she could look into a few possibilities and call her back soon.

"Call me whenever you find out anything," Myndi said. "No matter what time."

Myndi's hopes were rapidly diminishing. It was difficult to remain confident that somehow she would solve the mystery to the photo. She glanced up from the entries she'd been making in her journal and stared at the photograph of the woman and two children that she'd placed on her nightstand beside the photo of her mother and father. She wrote a final entry in her journal and then went to bed. She glanced one more time at the photo, but could only see her reflection before turning off the light and dropping off to sleep.

Myndi was startled awake by the ringing of her cell phone. It was just past midnight as she groped the surface of the nightstand trying to locate her phone.

"Hi, Myndi, sorry it's so late, but I had some thoughts about your mystery and wanted to run them by you," Krista said with excitement.

Myndi sat upright in bed. "Great, I'm all ears."

"Well, I've been dating a guy named Kyle for several months. He works at a telecommunications firm in Munich, and when I related your story to him, he was anxious to help. So today, Kyle's going to do some digging to see if he can find any leads through his company. Telecommunications is a big thing here in Germany. There's quite a grapevine, according to Kyle. Then, Myndi, I came up with a great idea," Krista said. "Why don't you come to Munich for a visit? You and I have communicated all these years but we've never met. You have time before you start teaching in the fall, and I have vacation days. It would be so much fun to finally meet you. What do you think? I'd love to show you Germany."

"Oh, Krista, that's a super idea. I have money left over from my graduation gifts and yes, there are still several weeks before I need to begin preparing lessons for my class. Let me do some digging, too," Myndi giggled.

"Okay, I need to return to work now so I'll talk with you later. Goodnight, Myndi!"

By the time Myndi made her way down to breakfast, she had already made the decision to take Krista up on her offer.

It was just after 7 a.m. when Myndi kissed her Grandma Kate good morning and discovered that the breakfast table had already been set up on the back porch sunroom for the two of them. The aroma of fresh brewed coffee and sunlight streaming in through the windows had always given Myndi a calm, cozy feeling.

"I thought you could use some cheering up this morning," smiled her grandmother. "You looked so disheartened last night, so I picked this bouquet of roses for you, honey," she whispered.

"Oh, they're lovely, Grandma. They still have dew on their petals and leaves."

Myndi sat down and sipped at her glass of orange juice. Their conversation centered on the photograph and Myndi reported what she and Krista had discussed at midnight.

They had almost finished breakfast when the phone rang. It was an excited Krista. "Myndi, I just got home from work and Kyle is here with me. We were planning on going out to dinner, but first Kyle has some exciting news to tell you. I'll put him on."

"Hi, Myndi," said Kyle in a heavy German accent. "I feel I know you already from all that Krista has told me." He laughed. "All good, of course."

"Hello, Kyle. I've heard some of you, too!" Myndi replied.

"Well, as Krista has told you, I also work in telecommunications. The same as you have discovered the occupation of the owner of the mysterious photo. Our company is very large and most of us commute to the office by train from nearby cities. I did a little digging today and came across an office memo that related a seminar that was held recently in Colorado, USA, for a group of senior advisors from our company. I checked the names of those in attendance at that conference and found the name of a Paul Kaufman. I do not know this Paul Kaufman personally, but I was able to speak with Mr. Kaufman's supervisor who told me that most of the employees had returned from the seminar, but that Paul Kaufman was taking an extended two-week holiday with his family. He's scheduled to return to work on Monday, July 12."

Myndi was pacing the floor with telephone at her ear while Kyle spoke.

"The best part," Kyle continued, "is that Mr. Kaufman's supervisor said Paul is married and he and his wife have two children, a son and a daughter. I looked in the company directory and found that they live in a small village very near the border of Switzerland, at Randegg, Germany, so the guy has quite a commute to work every day. But, of course, we have our fast trains. I've given Krista the address and telephone number for the Kaufman family. You two can work things out from here, I suspect."

"Oh, Kyle, I can't thank you enough!" choked Myndi, but by this time, Krista was back on the line.

"Krista! This is such good news just when I thought I'd reached all dead ends. I'm going to make arrangements this morning to book a flight to Germany. I'll try to fly into Munich. I'll let you know my itinerary just as soon as I can. I am so excited to see you and will be so happy to meet Kyle. Have a wonderful dinner. Love ya, Krista, Goodbye!"

Myndi was grinning as she hung up the phone and returned her attention to her grandmother. Kate had finished her breakfast and sat sipping her coffee while listening to the one-sided conversation where almost nothing had been said.

Myndi kissed her grandmother, then darted out of the sunroom shouting over her shoulder, "I'm going to Germany!"

Myndi placed a call to the Kaufman residence, thinking she would leave a message, but was surprised when a woman answered the phone.

"*Guten Tag.*"

"Oh! Hello! This is Myndi Carlson. I'm calling from the United States. May I speak with Mrs. Kaufman?"

Despite the heavy German accent, Myndi could understand the woman's reply. Although the woman spoke English, Myndi was thankful she had taken German as her foreign language in college.

"I am sorry to say Mrs. Kaufman is not here presently. The family is away on holiday. I am Gretchen, the nanny and housekeeper, staying in the home while they are away. The family is due to return on July 10, because Mr. Kaufman has to return to work the following Monday."

"I have a photograph that I think belongs to the Kaufmans," Myndi said. "Gretchen, do you think it would be possible to pay them a visit upon their return from holiday? I'd really like to deliver the photo in person."

"I think... no problem. I will let them know you called when I next speak with them."

"Thank you, Gretchen. I'll call back in a couple of days, after I've made my flight arrangements and know my itinerary."

Myndi hung up the phone and immediately placed a call to her friend, Sandy, a travel agent at "Let's Travel."

"Oh, Myndi, how exciting," Sandy exclaimed after hearing Myndi relate her story about finding the photograph. "When do you want to leave?"

"I know it's short notice, Sandy, but if there's a flight available to Munich on Saturday, July 3, that would be super and I'd like to return on July 15. I think that'll give me enough time. Did I tell you I will also be meeting the pen pal I've had since I was young? We've never met, and we're both really excited about it."

"Boy, Myndi, do you think that's enough time for everything you want to do while in Germany? It's such a wonderful country with so much to see and do."

"I know, Sandy, but I really need to get back and start preparing my sixth grade classroom for school in September."

"Myndi, while we've been talking, I checked on flights and you're in luck. I found a flight to Germany on July 3. It's an early flight out of Portland at 5 a.m. You'll have to make a connection in Dallas, Texas, for the flight to Munich and, of course, you'll need a passport and some kind of identification. The return flight from Munich is at 8 o'clock on the morning of July 15, their time. It's a straight through flight to Portland. Want me to book it while I'm here on line?"

"Yes, that'll be great, Sandy. Thanks so much. I'll

let you know about my trip when I return. We'll meet for lunch, okay?"

"Lunch is a deal, Myndi. So, you're all set. Have a safe flight and a lot of fun too. See you when you get back. You've sure got me curious."

I'm sure glad Jeff and I obtained passports for our short weekend trip to Canada last year, Myndi thought as she hung up the phone after giving Sandy her Visa charge card number. *And, I sure hope that'll give me enough time to meet the Kaufmans. But, if it doesn't work out, at least I'll have two weeks to spend with Krista!*

CHAPTER ELEVEN:

GERMANY

MYNDI ARRIVED IN MUNICH ON JULY 4. It had been an exhausting flight with little sleep due to vacationing families with small children, and the passenger seated next to her. When the man wasn't talking incessantly, he snored. Sometimes his head fell onto her shoulder and startled her. Plus, she had risen extremely early to catch the flight to Texas then had a three-hour layover before departing for Munich.

After retrieving her luggage at the baggage claim, and clearance through customs, Myndi made her way to the passenger arrival area. She looked around and hoped she would recognize Krista from her photos, but she chuckled when she saw a young woman hold a sign high above her head, waving it exuberantly—"MYNDI."

"I can't believe you're here, Myndi," choked an excited Krista as she hugged Myndi.

"I know. And I'm so happy to meet you after all these years, Krista."

"I've never been to the United States, or even on a long flight, but friends and relatives have said how tiring it can be. We'll go straight home so you can get a couple of hours nap. I've planned a quiet dinner for just the two of us. We can gab the night away, and then tomorrow, and for the next couple of days, I'll take you on a tour of my country."

The next five days were a whirlwind of sightseeing and excitement for Myndi. She sent postcards home to her grandmother from Munich, Heidelberg, and as far away as Frankfurt. They stayed at a bed and breakfast at a *gasthaus*, and ate a delicious German meal of sauerkraut and bratwurst in the evening. They stopped their road trip to take guided tours through numerous castles and cathedrals. They attended bier festivals and danced along with costumed folk singers. They cruised on the Rhine River, and even had lunch at an exquisite

French café near the German border. Myndi acquired a taste for German bier and *wiener schnitzel*. She couldn't get enough *apfelstrudel* served warm or cold, with ice cream or whipped cream, sometimes both. She collected recipes, took hundreds of photos, and gathered booklets and pamphlets from everywhere they visited. She sent Grandma Kate lots of postcards—sometimes as many as three in a day. She bought souvenirs to take back home, fell in love with Germany's flower—the beautiful Cyan Cornflower—and couldn't pass up buying herself a white tee-shirt with a bouquet of the blue flowers embroidered in the center of the front.

She met Kyle, Krista's boyfriend, at dinner one night and he took them to the famous Hofbrau Bierhaus in Munich, where they sang along to tunes played by the *oompah* band.

Myndi's journal entries sometimes ran on for multiple pages, and her anticipation of meeting with the Kaufmans grew more intense as the days passed.

The three-hour drive from Munich to Randegg seemed to drag, even though the scenery was outstanding. "This part of your country is reminiscent of the Western part of Oregon," she commented to Krista as they traveled.

It was 11 o'clock when Krista parked her auto in front of the Kaufman cottage, which had a stucco exterior embedded with wood slats placed at various levels and angles, and the bottom three feet rimmed with red brick as additional décor.

Myndi reached into the back seat and retrieved the wrapped photo along with two albums that held family snapshots.

"I'll wait for you here in the car, Myndi. Take your time. We have the rest of the day to play and we can spend the night at a *gasthaus* if you want to stay longer," Krista offered.

"You're welcome to come in with me, Krista. I might need some moral support."

"I'll be watching from here if you need me."

The long pathway to the house meandered through a meticulous flower garden. A cobblestoned pathway led Myndi to the front porch. The front door was oversized, with an oval window etched with a flower design. The glass in the window was beveled and frosted. Myndi banged the brass handle of the doorknocker, announcing her arrival. Her heart was pounding so hard she was afraid she might faint. She glanced back in Krista's direction and was reassured by the smile on her friend's face.

Myndi could hear the click of high heels and the voice of a woman calling out, "I'll get it, Gretchen." She heard the door lock unlatch and watched the doorknob turn. The door opened slowly....

There was an awkward moment and then both women gasped. They stood looking at each other, breathless, motionless, and dumbfounded to be looking at a face each had seen only in mirrors.

"Oh! Please forgive me. Come in, won't you? You must be Myndi Carlson. It appears we have a lot to talk about. I have a pot of tea brewing. My name is Madison, people call me Maddi."

"Yes," choked Myndi, taking a deep breath before asking, "Do you mind if my friend Krista comes in? I think it might be a long wait for her to sit alone in the car."

"By all means, have her come in. Please!" Maddi waved a welcome for Krista to come.

Maddi led them into a beautiful parlor. She introduced Gretchen when she entered the room bringing in a platter of scones and a cozy-wrapped teapot, which she set on the coffee table. Gretchen looked in awe at the identical faces.

"Where were you… born?" Myndi finished the sentence both she and Maddi had started in unison. "My father was in the Air Force. He and my mother lived in a home they rented while he was stationed at Bitburg Air Force Base, 22-years ago. Krista drove by it when we visited Frankfurt a couple days ago."

"Oh, my!" Maddi exclaimed. "So was I born at Bitburg?"

"You're twins!" shouted Krista, almost spilling her tea when she stood up just as Gretchen re-entered the room.

"You have a phone call, Madison."

"Tell them I'll call back later, Gretchen."

"But, it's your Aunt Patricia. She says it's very important."

"Excuse me for a moment while I take this call. My father is very ill. It may be a concern."

When Maddi returned to the parlor ten minutes later, she seemed excited. "That was my Aunt Patricia. She called to say my dad is having a good day today and she thinks we should pay him a visit. She's at the residential care home now and will greet us when we get there. It's only about fifteen minutes away. Please," she pleaded. "I don't know what's going on with Dad right now, but perhaps he can shed some light on what happened with us. My mother died two years ago, from cancer. Dad began his struggle with Alzheimer's two years before her death, but for a while, he was able to care for her. Aunt Patricia helped. I had my two young children, so it was a difficult time for all of us. I told Aunt Pat about your visit, Myndi."

"Then let's go," Myndi said, and they all immediately made their way to the door.

Fifteen minutes later, the three women arrived at the Rhinehaus Care Home and were introduced to Maddi's Aunt Patricia who was waiting for them in the lobby. She led them down a long corridor and into a hallway. Five doors down on the right they entered room 108.

Maddi was the first into the room and her father smiled broadly when she entered. He was seated in a large overstuffed chair near a picture window that had an iron bar exterior, but overlooked a lovely flower garden. With arms outstretched as Maddi approached, he gave her a long hug and kissed her gently on the cheek.

Maddi returned her father's embrace before moving aside to introduce his visitors. There was a moment of silence as the old man looked from his daughter to Myndi.

"Oh, no! Oh, no!" He covered his mouth, nose, and eyes to the scene. "I prayed this day would never come." He began to cry. "I thought I would perish before my horrible deed had been discovered." He spoke incoherently for a moment, then all of a sudden began screaming, "Nurse! Nurse! Come quickly! Someone help me! These people are attacking me! Get them out of here! Get them OUT OF HERE!"

The man continued screeching as Myndi and Krista fled the room, crossing paths with a nurse carrying a syringe.

It was twenty minutes before a teary-eyed Madison emerged from her father's room, followed closely by her Aunt Patricia.

"Please, if you don't mind, Myndi and Krista, will you return to Maddi's?" Aunt Patricia said. "I'll join you as soon as I can. Chris has had a bad setback because of my insisting that you come today. I had no idea this would happen, but I think I can shed some light on the past. I might have answers to the myriad of questions going through your minds right now."

On the way back to the Kaufman's home, Myndi related her early childhood—the death of her parents and being raised by her grandparents. She continued her story when they returned to the Kaufman's parlor. Madison sat motionless. Tears ran down and streaked her cheeks.

Gretchen appeared with a fresh pot of hot tea

and soon after that, Maddi's Aunt Patricia arrived. When she walked in, the two women were standing in an embrace, trying without success to console each other.

Aunt Patricia suggested they all sit down. She said she had a story to relate.

"Two years ago, when your mother was diagnosed with cancer, Maddi, and the doctors confirmed there was no cure, she pleaded with your father to write a letter of explanation to you. I was there because Chris was already in his second year of Alzheimer's and getting worse. But he begged me and your mother to let the story of what they had done, the lies they had told, die with them. But, your mother, Chris's sister, Betsy, pleaded and finally won out. I didn't know the whole story then, only that whatever it was had eaten at them for years. Chris asked me to leave the room. 'Pat,' he said, 'Betsy and I want to write a letter of confession. And we want you to hold the letter in strict secrecy until we have both passed on.'

"Because the two of them were so distraught, I

made the promise and later that same day, Chris gave me a sealed envelope. He made me repeat my promise to never reveal the contents of the letter to anyone until after the two of them had died.

"Well, when Maddi told me of your impending visit, Myndi, and something about a photograph that you'd found and wanted to return in person— my curiosity got the better of me. Not to mention that I, too, had some questions that had preyed on my mind for years—about the birth of Maddi." Aunt Patricia swallowed hard and moved over to take a seat next to Maddi.

"So, last week, when Chris was going through another very bad spell, and with your impending visit, Myndi, God forgive me, I broke the seal on the letter and read... the confession."

CHAPTER TWELVE:

THE CONFESSION

Dear Maddi,

At one time long ago, your mother and I decided that ours was a story we hoped would never have to be told. But now that Betsy is so ill and no cure for her cancer seems to be in sight, and because I have been diagnosed with Alzheimer's disease, we know there might come a time when you will need answers. Your Aunt Patricia has kept this letter in strict confidence. I made her promise not to open the letter until after both your mother and I have passed away. I will try to keep this letter to the point and I apologize for the pain it may cause you, my dear daughter.

If you are reading this letter, then it appears that time has come.

Your mother and I had been married for fifteen years. Your mother was 40 years old and I was 43. All our married life we had tried to have children, but found we were infertile. I was a general practitioner; your mother was a nurse. We had our own practice, located just outside the Bitburg Air Force Base.

Throughout the years, I watched your mother suffer every time she held another woman's baby. I'd see the pain in her eyes when we'd pass by a school or park where children swung on swings, or when we'd hear their giggles as they slid down slides or played on teeter-totters or merry-go-rounds.

I couldn't stand seeing her pain. I prayed for a way to make her happy, knowing our only option was to have a child of our own.

One day I received a call from the Air Force Medical Department at Bitburg. One of their jets had crashed and all their medical teams were tied up, desperately trying to save the eight crewmembers on that plane.

The call I received concerned an Air Force officer whose wife was about to deliver their first child. No one else was around, so the officer in charge requested my assistance. He asked if I would deliver their child in the birthing room at my clinic. Of course I agreed to their request.

Within an hour, the young mother-to-be arrived in our office and Betsy and I attended to her while she was in labor. The labor was a long one, lasting almost six hours. She was exhausted by then.

All during her pregnancy only been one heartbeat had been heard by the Air Force doctors, which is not unusual for twins, especially identical twins, and is also dependent on their position in the womb. But I heard two heartbeats.

So please forgive me, but I had a plan. As I said previously, your mother had become more distraught every year due to her longing for a child of her own.

Betsy and I were alone with the woman delivering the child. Her husband was off on a mission and not due back for several days. Two beautiful identical twin girls were born, six minutes apart.

I take the blame for hiding you away and making the parents and everyone else believe that there had been only one baby born to that couple. It was easy enough to do: I just sent one child home with Betsy and continued to care for the mother and infant until the Air Force Medical team sent an ambulance to take the two of them back to the base hospital.

No one asked any questions. I filled out the necessary papers and five months *after the birth, the young man and his family were sent stateside to fulfill the remainder of his Air Force contract.*

I closed my medical practice in Bitburg one month after you were born and we moved to Munich. I had never seen your mother so happy and content. You were her life. You were our life. We lavished attention on you and loved you with all our hearts.

Secretly, I kept track of the young Air Force family and was devastated to learn of an automobile accident that took the lives of the couple and their son. I never revealed any of this to Betsy.

But you accomplished all our hopes and dreams. All I wanted in life was Betsy's happiness. Forgive me!

Patricia was my only sibling and your mother had none. Our parents, your grandparents, had all died within a few years of each other before you were born.

Patricia lived in France at the time and because she was busy raising her own children, we hadn't seen her in several years. So when she heard the news that Betsy had delivered a baby girl, she was elated and happy for us. All she knew was that we had been trying our entire married life to conceive, and that now our prayers were answered.

Patricia, you now know the secret we have harbored all these years. You will be reading this letter after my death. And Maddi, I hope and pray you will not harbor ill of us. We loved you as our own.

Someday, God willing, you may search and hopefully find your identical twin sister. I understand that she has been raised by her loving grandparents.

I am including with this letter a copy of your true birth certificate and the last known address of the grandparents of your twin sister—they named her Myndi.

I hope the love we had as a family, the love you have shown us as our child, and the memories we've made together will see you through any heartaches you may have after you read this confession.

Finally, I pray that God, in all his mercy, will forgive us, especially me because it was my insistence that Betsy live my lie.

With all our love forever and always, dear daughter.

—Mom and Dad

The silence in the room during Patricia's reading of the letter suddenly erupted into sobs from all four. Maddi and Myndi's tears were almost unbearable for Krista to witness. The sisters held each other and, as the minutes passed, the sobs diminished, bringing silence once again.

"Thank you, Aunt Patricia," said Maddi as she turned and reached for Myndi's hand. "This is so utterly unbelievable and yet so wonderful. It saddens me that this ever happened, but I was never mistreated by my mother and father. They loved me so much and showed it throughout my whole life."

"Of course, I understand, Maddi." Myndi smiled as she wiped the tears from her face. "But, we have the rest of our lives now to make up for lost time and I am so thankful for the journey that led me to the pho...."

"Mommy! Mommy!" a voice shouted from the hallway. Myndi could hear small feet padding toward the parlor. "Whose car is that in front? Do we have company?"

"Yes, Caroline, we do have company, honey."

Maddi called back, rushing to the parlor door and intercepting her children—four-year-old Caroline and two-year-old Ryan. "And I have a great surprise for the two of you in the other room. Mommy found out today that she has a sister who has been living in America ever since we were born. She is my identical twin and she is waiting to greet you both. It's a long story, but first come and meet your Aunt Myndi."

Maddi then looked up at her husband, Paul, who had just come through the front door with an armload of groceries.

"Ah, so I see your visitor has arrived," Paul said.

"Oh, Paul, you won't believe what happened. But first, I have to introduce you and the children to Myndi. Come with me, children," Maddi said as she led them into the parlor. Paul followed close behind.

Both children buried their faces in their mother's skirt after spotting Myndi.

"It's okay," whispered Myndi as she knelt and reached her arms out for Caroline and Ryan. "I know you're surprised that I look just like your mom, and I was surprised too. But after a lifetime not knowing each other existed, we've finally found each other. Please come and give your Aunt Myndi a hug."

It took Paul a minute to recover, but he didn't know what to say, so he just reassured the children. "It's okay, kids. Isn't Aunt Myndi beautiful?" He smiled a sheepish grin at Maddi.

"I can see there's a lot for all of you to talk about," said Krista. "I'm going head down the street to the *gasthaus* we spotted on the way over. I'll make a reservation for us to stay overnight, or should we plan to stay the rest of the week? Your plane doesn't leave until early on the fifteenth, so we have four days to spend in Randegg, if you want."

"Oh! No! We wouldn't hear of it. You can stay here, in the guest bedroom. Don't you think?" Maddi raised an eyebrow in Paul's direction.

"By all means! Please stay. There are so many unanswered questions and so much catching up for the two of you," Paul stated.

Myndi nodded her head, yes, toward a waiting Krista, who also agreed.

Gretchen came into the room. "May I serve lunch on the back porch patio, Madison?" she inquired.

"Oh, my goodness it's way past time for lunch," said Maddi. "There'll be seven of us, Gretchen, including the children. They can take their naps after lunch, okay?"

"Super," stated Krista. "I'll get our luggage then."

"Here, let me help," offered Paul.

Maddi waited at the bottom of the stairs with Myndi. Paul handed the suitcase he carried into the house to Myndi, and the three women made their way upstairs.

"Oh! What a beautiful room." Krista said as she touched her hand to the blue goose down coverlet on the oversized bed. Myndi walked to the window framed with light blue nylon panels. Outside was the strikingly beautiful landscaped backyard.

"How lovely," Myndi exclaimed as she squeezed Maddi's hand. "This is exquisite."

"I have lunch set up," called Gretchen from the bottom of the staircase. "How does bratwurst on my homemade bread, with chocolate cake for dessert sound? Well," she giggled, "that's what I'm serving."

Chapter Thirteen:

Getting Acquainted

THE NEXT FOUR DAYS WERE SPENT with Myndi and Maddi relating childhood stories and going over photo albums Maddi brought down from the den.

The young women discovered that their grades in school were similar, although Myndi learned the German school system seemed superior to her experience in the United States.

"I met Paul in my ninth year at school. He was in his final year of high school at that time. When he graduated from college, where he'd been studying engineering, and secured a good job, we got married. I was only seventeen. Caroline came along ten months later. I had planned to attend college, but decided to stay home to be with her. She was two years old when Ryan came along, but I still wanted to continue my education. So, we hired Gretchen and she has been a jewel. I'm able to go to school full time, and by this time next year, Myndi, I'll be able to apply for a job at the same grade school I attended as a child."

"Oh, Maddi, I will start my first year of teaching in September."

Their remaining days together were filled with conversations that illuminated coincidences between their two lives. They had both worn braces during their tenth through thirteenth years. Both contracted measles and chicken pox when they were eight. Both had always worn their auburn hair long, and sometimes in a ponytails. They both took music lessons, first on the clarinet, and then the saxophone, when they were nine years old. They had the same favorite foods, and the same foods they disliked. Their favorite color was blue. They were even the same religion.

And, oddly enough, when Myndi explained about the accident that took the life of their birth parents and her brother, Bobby, Maddi related how she had broken her ankle and had to have a cast on her leg during the summer months, when she was only five years old.

On the morning of July 14, Myndi and Krista packed their luggage before coming down the stairs for breakfast.

"Here, let me give you a hand with those bags," Paul said. "I'll take them out to the car and meet you in the kitchen. Maddi and the children are waiting for you."

Myndi couldn't help but notice a strange look on Paul's face. She searched for an explanation, but soon his expression changed to a wide grin. He turned away, carrying the suitcases out the front door. She thought she heard him laugh as he shut the door behind him.

The breakfast table was set with china that had a light blue flower pattern. The children were already seated at the table.

"*Guten Morgen*, Auntie Myndi," they shouted in unison and then scrambled down from their chairs running to embrace Myndi and Krista.

Maddi emerged from the pantry just as Paul returned from the car. He was still grinning. But he laughed loudly when he saw Myndi's mouth gape open as she gazed at Maddi.

The twins were dressed in the same tee shirt Myndi had picked up at the shop in Munich, when she visited there with Krista. Everyone laughed as the sisters hugged and began to tear up, as they had done so many times during the past three days.

It was a tearful goodbye as Myndi and Krista walked down the front steps and long the path to Krista's car.

Myndi looked back through the rear window as Maddi, Paul, and the children waved goodbye.

CHAPTER FOURTEEN:

EPILOG

THE FIVE YEARS SINCE MYNDI'S DISCOVERY of the photo that led to her finding her identical twin sister flew by. Myndi had filled five more journals recording the excitement of her first year of teaching sixth grade students, and of her marriage to Jeff. Maddi had served as Matron of Honor. Paula and her husband drove in from Kellogg, Idaho.

Although Myndi and Paula had made a childhood pact to be each other's Maids of Honor, Paula was happy to concede the role to Maddi. And Krista had been delighted to accept the role of Myndi's second Bride's Maid. Krista flew in from Germany on the same flight as Maddi, Paul, Caroline, and Ryan.

Grandma Kate was beside herself when meeting

her granddaughter, Maddi, for the first time. Myndi watched the instant love form between them.

The month-long honeymoon after their wedding took up almost half her journal that year. And the next four years were filled with multiplication— their daughter Karylynn was born the following June, and two years later Myndi gave birth to Robert, who everyone called Bobby.

Myndi's latest entry in her journal was full of the exciting news that their house was finally complete. It seemed like all her dreams were coming true.

Paul's firm in Germany was transferring him to the United States. He would be the manager of the Engineering Department at a high-tech firm in the Beaverton area of Oregon, a fifteen-minute drive from the home where Myndi and her family resided. Just another coincidence.

It was evening, and Myndi was sitting at her vanity, combing her long auburn hair. Pausing for a moment, she reached for the photo that she'd found at the Holiday Inn in Steamboat Spring's all those years ago. She smiled at the image of her sister, niece, and nephew. Caroline was just four years old back then, and Ryan only two. Gently she replaced the framed photograph on its permanent spot on her dresser. Then she held up the photo of herself with her two children taken when Karylynn was four, and Bobby was two. Bobby had been named in honor of her own little brother.

Between the two pictures was a photograph of her parents. Myndi smiled at the fourth framed image—her wedding photo. Jeff was so incredibly handsome standing there by her side.

Her thoughts drifted to the conversation she'd had with Paula all those years ago. Recently Paula said, "Jason is still the same old cad he's always been… one trophy female after another."

"Myndi!" Grandma Kate hollered from the bottom of the staircase, breaking Myndi's reverie. "Jeff is waiting in the car. Hurry up! He needs to drop you off at school."

Myndi smiled one last time at her reflection.

CAST:
(IN ORDER OF APPEARANCE)

Myndi—the main character of this story

Grandma Kathryn—Myndi's grandmother, Kate

Jeff—Myndi's fiancé

Ginger—Myndi's dog

Paula—Myndi's friend in Kellogg, Idaho

Jason—the man Myndi dated in Kellogg, Idaho

Paul Kaufman—Maddi's husband

Krista—Myndi's pen pal in Germany

Kyle—Krista's boyfriend

Gretchen—Maddi's housekeeper

Madison (Maddi)—Myndi's twin sister

Patricia—Maddi's aunt

Betsy—Maddi's mother

Chris—Maddi's father

Caroline—Maddi's daughter

Ryan—Maddi's son

Robert (Bobby) —Myndi's son

Karylynn—Myndi's daughter

ABOUT THE AUTHOR

During the fall of 2008, at the insistence of her husband and children, **Joan (Michalke) Ritchey** was persuaded to publish her first book of poetry and prose, *From Him... Through My Fingertips.* The book is a collection of poems and short stories written over a thirty-year period. "The thrill of seeing my words in print was the most fun I've ever had."

Since 2003, Joan has taken numerous writing classes and attended many writing seminars. In addition, she's become an active member of several writing/critique groups and has participated in open-mic readings, all of which have helped develop the writing skills she chose to forgo in high school—majoring instead in business education (typing and shorthand).

Joan's thrill of writing continued, and in 2012, her novel, *The Brooch*, was published by Dancing Moon Press. Joan chuckled when a peer said, "Characters in stories come alive as you write. They dictate the story to you." A skeptic at the time, Joan now says, "Believe it! The characters *do* take over."

In her third book, *Captured Reflections*, Joan ventured even deeper into poetry—accepting challenges by others, attempting various formal poetic forms and light verse. The short stories include fiction as well as non-fiction.

This book, *Coincidences*, is a novel full of hints that lead to an intriguing conclusion. What fun!